# KRONK

The river stank. It stank of time, effluent and the subtle odours of twelve million Londoners. Nevertheless, in the half-light there was a hint of mystery—nay, even magic—on the waters of the Thames. Not enough mystery or magic to inspire one to leap off the bridge without further consideration. But at least enough to make one consider the possibility. Calmly and without haste. The question was whether he would drown first or be poisoned by the toxic waste that, over a few decades, had transformed the Thames into a rich brown syrup. Perhaps all that industrial crap had altered the river's specific gravity. Perhaps he would simply float like a cork until he died of horror at the variety of unmentionables—even unthinkables— drifting past his nose.

His meditations were interrupted by a bra.

**Also by the same author,
and available in Coronet Books:**

# Kronk

---

# Edmund Cooper

**CORONET BOOKS**
Hodder and Stoughton

Copyright © 1970 by Edmund Cooper

First published 1970 by
Hodder and Stoughton Ltd as SON OF KRONK

Coronet edition 1972
*Third impression 1978*

———————————————————

Printed and bound in Great Britain for
Hodder and Stoughton Paperbacks,
a division of Hodder and Stoughton Ltd.,
Mill Road, Dunton Green, Sevenoaks, Kent
(Editorial Office: 47 Bedford Square, London, WC1 3DP)
by Richard Clay (The Chaucer Press), Ltd.,
Bungay, Suffolk

ISBN 0 340 16217 1

*All is for the best in the best of all possible worlds.*

VOLTAIRE

# CHAPTER ONE

Armed with a half-litre bottle of British vodka, two plastic cups and the conviction that suicide would be an appropriate conclusion to his artistic non-career, Gabriel Crome sat on the steps of the Albert Memorial and felt sad.

He had said goodbye to all his favourite landmarks. The Albert Memorial, being the most hideous and therefore the most attractive, was the last.

It was always last; for Gabriel was subjected to his suicide kick with about the same degree of regularity that a healthy child-bearing woman is subjected to ovulation. He recognized the symptoms—headache, tension and a screaming desire to withdraw from the messy cycle of existence. One of these days, he told himself gloomily, the ovum of despair would really be fertilized by his wriggling death-wish. And darkness would lie upon the face of the shallow.

Meanwhile, there was the vodka, the ritual, the angst and

the raven. He did not know whether the raven was a permanent squatter in the memorial, an incarnation of Prince Albert or the familiar spirit of all pseudo-suicides. He knew only that it was always there whenever he was and that the wisdom of its silence was only equalled by the wisdom of its utterances on the tragic pattern of existence.

Recently, Gabriel had formed the habit of bringing two plastic cups to the Albert Memorial. He could not remember when he had first begun to corrupt the raven, but it was now well on the way to becoming an alcoholic.

"*Salud*," said Gabriel. "A non-death is as unsatisfactory as a non-life, do you not think? Presently, I shall wend—not entirely devoid of hope—to Waterloo Bridge to see if my luck has changed. Meanwhile, bird of ill-omen, frowzy fowl, let us drink the juice that dulls the edge of dullness." He hiccupped, then slopped more vodka into the plastic cups.

The raven approached warily. It had grown accustomed to Gabriel's tirades. Sometimes, he was wont to indulge in sudden disquieting gestures. But the bird was in no position to choose its drinking companions. Gabriel was not only its corrupter but also its only supplier.

"Ha, bird," snapped Gabriel, "you think I'm pissed already?"

The raven offered no comment. It dipped its beak in the vodka, flung back its head like a Russian to the manner born, and swallowed, opening and closing the beak several times, as if this was the nearest it could get to smacking its lips. The performance was repeated.

"You are right, little brother," went on Gabriel. "I am pissed. In fact, I am—by St. Ringo—a litre ahead of you. Furthermore, I propose to stay that way . . . There is a gulf between us, little brother, a million years wide and a hundred proof deep. I have a soul: you have not. All you have are bloody feathers, pure subjectivity, and a psyche that cannot even contemplate mañana . . . That's my trouble, birdie. I can think of the morrow. I can even remember yesterday. Which is why I wish I were dead."

There were tears in Gabriel's eyes; but he was not yet maudlin enough to want to shed them.

"What are you, bastard bird?" he demanded aggressively. The raven did not answer. It was too busy drinking.

So Gabriel answered his own question. "You are nothing but a bastard bird. Whereas I, Gabriel Crome, schizoid of this parish, am demonstrably human. Which is to say ambitious, which is to say frustrated. I think, therefore I wish to cease to exist. The world is my oyster—but I do not know how to open oysters. Big joke."

The raven drank some more. Then it staggered a little and uttered. It said quite clearly: "Kronk!"

"True, indeed," said Gabriel, raising his own cup. "True indeed. The apocalyptic verdict. I do not know how to open oysters. Kronk! I do not even know if there are any oysters worth opening. Kronk! I want recognition. Kronk! I want someone to love. Kronk! And, failing all that, I just want to bleeding die."

"Kronk," said the raven once more.

"You are so right," said Gabriel. "A meaningful comment not only on my predicament but on the basic tragedy of our time. Artists are suspect, love is redundant, people are obsolete. Consumers are all." He took another swallow of vodka. "I am a consumer, yes. But I am more than the sum of my consumptions. I am an artist, a book sculptor. And, since no one wishes to acquire a 1984 edition of the Encyclopaedia Britannica translated—with the aid of two pounds of flour, a pint of water and a roll of Sellotape—into Leda and the Swan, I wish to die. It is symptomatic of the age, dear raven. Michelangelo is without honour in his own credit rating. From them that hath not shall be taken away."

Gabriel gazed at Albert, sitting on his throne in the memorial. The long summer twilight, the balmy air and the effect of seventy-five proof vodka endowed the petrified royal consort with an illusion of life, a suggestion of movement. Gabriel thought he saw him wink.

"And the same to you, sweet prince . . . You have got it manufactured, haven't you, cocky? Sitting up there, watching the rest of us trolley off to the paper dolly farm or get stoned out of our trees . . . All those children. I have often wondered. Was little Vicky a beautifully bouncy lover, or was there no other outlet for all that royal creative energy? No offence, old sport. Just claim the fifth amendment. By all that is whiter than white, I wish I were you. Dead and dynastic and nirvanic on a cold backside. No matter. I am not Albert the Good. I am Gabriel the superfluous. Such is the whim of time, chromosomes and carelessly opened legs."

There was still some vodka left in the bottle. Gabriel glanced at the raven's cup then poured the remains of the vodka into his own. The bird stared at him, he thought, somewhat reproachfully.

"Bird," said Gabriel severely, "do not presume upon a chance acquaintance. You are nothing to me. I am nothing to you. Yet I am comforted by the fact that when I finally scramble the transistors between my ears, there will be someone who mourns. Will you get the shakes, you feathery fantast? Will you fall about in front of Albert, croaking for a large vodka? And how, dependent creature, will you tell the other tourists that all you need is a fix? Well, these are your problems, you fat black feather bag. Pray for me. I go to see if there are any vacant appointments in Samarra."

The raven's legs gave way. There was a subdued gurgling in its throat; but the bird refrained from further comment. It flopped helplessly as Gabriel walked down the steps from the Albert Memorial with care and concentration. Then, as if in seeing its guest off the premises it had concluded its final duty as host, the raven keeled over and slept.

## CHAPTER TWO

The noble youth standing in the centre of Waterloo Bridge
on the right pedway was ten foot tall. He had long, splendid
hair, divinely sensuous lips and a pelvic tilt that was out of
this world. He stared down the river with the intensity of
one looking for an armada that was several centuries over-
due. He was made of bronze.

Gabriel looked at the inscription on the plinth.

In Palace Script, it read: Sir Michael Jagger, Bart.

Underneath that, in Old English Text, there was: Let
him that is without sin cast the first Stone.

And underneath that was: Jacovus Bierstein facit.

Gabriel followed the glance of Sir Michael Jagger, Bart.
The river stank. It stank of time, effluent and the subtle
odours of twelve million Londoners. Nevertheless, in the
half-light there was a hint of mystery—nay, even magic—on
the waters of the Thames. Not enough mystery or magic to

inspire one to leap off the bridge without further consideration. But at least enough to make one consider the possibility.
Calmly and without haste. The question was whether he
would drown first or be poisoned by the toxic waste that,
over a few decades, had transformed the Thames into a rich
brown syrup. Perhaps all that industrial crap had altered
the river's specific gravity. Perhaps he would simply float like
a cork until he died of horror at the variety of unmentionables—even unthinkables—drifting past his nose.

The theory of suicide was excellent: the hard facts were
simply repellent. Better to get drunk, take pills and go to
sleep in a warm bath. Provided one could be sure of not
waking up shivering and with a hangover.

His meditations were interrupted by a bra.

It fell on his shoulder, and it seemed to come from the
direction of Sir Michael Jagger, Bart. Though, hitherto, the
statue had not displayed any transvestite tendencies. The bra
was followed by some lace nonsense and the sound of
sneezing.

Gabriel walked round the statue. A dark-haired girl of
perhaps twenty-three or twenty-five, clad only in fishnet
tights, was tying a rope round her neck. The rope was not
very long. Its other end was tied securely to an old five-kilo
weight resting on the parapet of the bridge. The rest of the
girl's clothing was strewn on the pedway.

"Good evening," said Gabriel. "A trifle warm for the time
of year, don't you think? I hope I am not intruding."

"Please go away. I'm busy." Her voice shook a little, but
otherwise sounded quite normal.

"I don't wish to intrude. But we seem to have a mutual
interest. However, the river stinks, the time is out of joint,
and I am sure you would not wish to swallow unwholesome
semi-solids."

She shuddered. Gabriel repressed a feeling of triumph.

15

She could easily leap on the parapet and kick the five-kilo weight over before a vodka-stricken non-hero had time to intervene.

"Please go away. My husband is dead, I have a dread disease and I do not wish the bounty hunters to get any of my body."

"Self-pity," said Gabriel, taking another cautious step, "is a destroyer of perspective. As my dear mother at the Yurkuti Embassy used to say, there are few problems that cannot be resolved by a bottle, a tumble, a cup of tea or a good night's sleep . . . Unfortunately, having emptied the bottle and enjoyed the tumble, she accidentally electrocuted herself while making a cup of tea prior to a good night's sleep. The Yurkuti flags were flown at half mast for twenty-one days. I still have not got over her loss."

The girl burst out laughing. "I don't believe the Yurkuti Embassy exists."

Gabriel shrugged, and took another step. "If it did not, it would have been necessary to invent it. My mother existed, though. When she was fifty-three, she thought it was all a great drag. So she flipped to Munich for the Oktoberfest, had a twenty-four carat time and at the end sold her body for twenty-thousand D marks. I had the D marks and she had the last laugh. They found one diseased kidney, cancer of the lung and a heart with about as much mileage in it as a nineteen-twenty Rolls. The eyes were good, though. Her eyes were always good."

He grabbed the girl, holding her fiercely and idiotically. One moment she had been trying to commit suicide, the next moment she had managed a laugh, and now she was sobbing fit to burst. Some spinhead.

And why should Gabriel Crome, cretin at large, book sculptor without patrons, suicide pretender and amateur alcoholic, step round Sir Michael Jagger to save an adult female from the Thames? Something required to be examined. Possibly, the whole of human history.

"My name is Gabriel Crome," he said gently. "I undertake not to bore, beat or ravish you until we are in a better place and in better states of mind. I am a failed book sculptor and a failed suicide. Please forgive my intrusion. It is probably entirely due to masculine pride. One simply hates to see a woman succeed."

She continued to sob with verve and decibels, while Gabriel continued to hold her tightly, convinced that she had not heard a word he had spoken. Naturally, he was wrong. Presently, the sobbing subsided somewhat; and a breast twitched with brief indiscretion against his ribs. He smiled. She was beginning to recall the facts of life once more.

"I have made an idiot of myself," she said. "Forgive me. I think I had better dress."

"There is no hurry. I like you as you are."

"Possibly. But what of the procs?"

Bang on cue, there was the high whine of a hover sled upon the otherwise deserted bridge. It moaned to a halt, then hissed and clanked as the air-cushion died and the sled sank to the pedway.

Two uniformed proctors leaped off the sled. One grabbed the girl and the other squirted an aerosol pencil of freezair into Gabriel's face.

Gabriel froze. He had no option. The muscles of his body seized and went rigid, as if they had just been dipped in liquid oxygen. He could still think, though. And feel.

He felt considerably as the proctor hit his face three times then prodded him with a jump wand for good measure. The electric shock seemed to echo round his body like thunder in deserted alleyways. He wanted to scream. He would have been very grateful for the opportunity to scream. But the freezair wouldn't let him. It wouldn't even let him die mentally. He began to think that there were worse conditions to be in than floating with unmentionables and unthinkables down the Thames.

"What's this? What's this? What's this?" demanded the proctor who had snatched the girl from Gabriel's arms. His hand lingered accidentally but tenderly over one of her erect if confused nipples. "Rape? Assault? Attempted murder? Coercion? Grievous bodily? You name it, darling. We make this boyo bounce like a butyl ball."

"Please!" she said tearfully, "please. He was helping me. He just saved my life."

Both proctors registered the rope and the five-kilo weight. Balloons formed over their heads.

"Excreta!" said Proc One.

"Plus derision," said Proc Two. He regarded the girl sternly. "You high?"

"Certainly not," she snapped with indignation. "Unhappy only. I have a right to be unhappy, have I not?"

"Yes, darling."

"There is no law against *felo de se*?"

"No, darling. But there are three thousand nine hundred and seventy-two laws against stripping on the king's highway, which this happens to be, with intent. And they are practically all capital offences . . . Let me see. We could pull you on intent to riot, disturbing the king's peace, soliciting, obstruction, vagrancy, bribery—since what you're showing constitutes bribery—loitering, distracting proctors from their duty, psychopathic action, sedition and wilfully perverting the course of justice . . . Namepad, darling, and think yourself lucky if we don't call a funny wagon."

She began to cry again.

"Cut the commercial," said Proc One. "Give with the newsflash."

"Camilla Greylaw," she said. "Box 1735, Babscastle Boulevard, Hampstead. My husband—at least, he was until the day before yesterday—is, I mean was, Professor Greylaw, late of the Microbiological Warfare Divison of the Ministry of International Security and Race Harmony. If you wish any further information I will give it only after I have contacted my solicitors, Haroun al Raschid and Co., King's Road, Chelsea."

"Ho," said Proc One. He slapped Gabriel's face again. Gabriel tried to blink and couldn't. "Who is the rigid Galahad, then?"

"I don't know."

"Ah, you don't know." He took another aerosol pencil from his belt and squirted Gabriel's face.

Gabriel sneezed. Movement was restored to his muscles. He willed himself not to hit anybody.

"Well, student?" demanded Proc Two enigmatically. He tapped his jump wand, reminding Gabriel of its possibilities.

"I am not a student."

"Namepad."

"Gabriel Crome, Top C 13, Queensway Village, West 2."

"So, angel. What do you do on a good day?"

"Teach a raven to get drunk at the Albert Memorial."

The jump wand touched him, and a further shot of high voltage plucked at his nerves and muscles. Gabriel bit his tongue. It didn't do any good. He still roared with pain.

"Now tell us about the bad days, little one."

"I—I'm a book sculptor." The wand moved. He gazed at it with some apprehension, then added quickly: "I make sculpture out of books—models, figures, every damn thing."

"Francis," said Proc One to his companion, "I'm bored. Do we hit these infants or don't we?"

"Good cue," responded the other proctor. He seemed uncertain for a moment or two, then he said: "We don't. While we play with the funnies, goddam students probably lifting the dome off St. Paul's." He turned to Camilla and Gabriel. "Pray for us, children. This is your lucky evening . . . And, darling, draw a veil over those lovely boobs. The scene is disturbing for all virtuous citizens. Further, go home. You should both know that darkness brings out the big bad boys."

"Thank you, officer," said Camilla gently.

"Thank you, officer," said Gabriel, wishing that he had a flamethrower.

The proctors mounted their sled. The air-cushion lifted it clear of the pedway. It hurtled across the bridge towards the West End.

"Did it hurt much?" asked Camilla.

"Yes."

"I'm sorry. It was all my fault."

"Not entirely. It serves me right for not jumping. Now, you really had better dress—and don't say another word about procs. I've had my quota for one day. A short time ago, I was nicely stoned. Now I'm sober enough to want to smash the human race."

Camilla began to do interesting and womanly things, all of which conspired to rapidly cover the warm, dusky beauty of her torso. "Will you come home with me?" she asked. "I mean, I'm lonely and there are the cats to feed, and Eustace isn't going to be there any more, and I want to talk to someone because I don't know what to do."

"I will come home with you," said Gabriel, eying her with approval, "because I also am lonely, and though I have no cats to feed and no Eustace to miss, I still don't know what to do."

"You shall listen," said Camilla almost gaily. "And I will tell you about Eustace and the dread disease. Then you shall help me feed the cats . . . I hope you won't mind the smell."

"Who knows?" said Gabriel. "There may be compensations."

# CHAPTER THREE

They fed the cats. But before they did so, Gabriel received one or two interesting surprises.

1735, Babscastle Boulevard, was not an apartment as he had imagined. It was a large, detached house, mid-twentieth century rococo, standing in its own grounds surrounded by high walls. It must have cost the late Professor Eustace Greylaw a stack to buy or even rent the place. Maybe he'd been a forger, or a Member of Parliament, or even a bounty hunter.

Camilla led the way up the drive and placed her thumb in the id ring. The front door opened.

There, waiting to greet her, was a Bengal tiger. To Gabriel, it suddenly seemed as if suicide was no longer a matter for serious decision-making. Camilla, however, remained unagitated. So did the tiger. A grey squirrel sat calmly on its back, cracking a hazel nut.

"Hi, Diddums," said Camilla. "You missed me, didn't you, fat old pussy? Say hello to the nice gentleman who snatched me from the Thames."

The squirrel cracked the hazel nut. The tiger purred and held out its paw.

"Diddums likes you," said Camilla.

"I like Diddums," croaked Gabriel, the sweat pouring down his face. He had read somewhere—probably in an old book he had been sculpting—that animals could smell fear.

With supreme courage, he put out his hand and shook the extended paw. The tiger opened his mouth and yawned. Gabriel fainted. When next he returned to consciousness, cushions had been placed under his head and Camilla was trying to get him to drink something.

He held the attention of an admiring audience. One tiger, one squirrel, one lion, one lamb, one panther and one fat white rabbit. He tried to faint again, but without success.

"I should have told you," said Camilla. "How stupid of me. I should have told you. But I wanted it to be a surprise."

"It was a surprise," admitted Gabriel. "Yes, there was definitely the element of surprise." He recovered sufficiently to sit up.

Camilla looked at the ring of animals. "Go away! Shoo! Shoo! The gentleman and I want to talk to each other without being interrupted by silly creatures like you. Go on, all of you, back to the basement."

She drove the animals from the room. The lamb bleated, one of the cats sneezed with subdued thunder. Then there was the sound of a closing door.

Gabriel got to his feet and looked around. He was in what had once been a rather splendidly furnished room. But there were tooth marks on the grand piano and rabbit droppings on the unchewed sections of the Indian carpet. The long tapestry curtains by the french windows hung in tattered rags.

The settee and easy chairs also had not been greatly improved by the frolicking of the big cats; and the squirrel, evidently, had chosen to secrete various hoards of nuts in the most improbable places.

Camilla returned. "I have left the garden door open so they can get a bit of exercise . . . Now, we'll have a drink and a talk. You will help me to feed them, won't you? I simply don't like handling lumps of raw meat."

"Whether I help you or not really depends on how convincing your story is. At the moment, as an ex-suicide I just feel very lucky to be still alive."

"The procs introduced us, so I shall call you Gabriel and you shall call me Camilla. They are rather nice names. We should have met about two years ago, before I knew Eustace. Will you stay with me tonight? Do you drink whisky? Oh, and what is a book sculptor? It sounds dreadfully clever."

"Do you always fire questions in salvoes?"

She laughed. "I'm sorry. Eustace used to say that I reminded him of Marilyn Monroe with a black thatch."

"Eustace couldn't have been that old."

"He was, nearly. I mean he was about fifty years older than me. That's why he married me—because I reminded him of Marilyn Monroe. He had tapes of all those quaint old movies I think they worked on him like an aphrodisiac or something because he always—what did you say about the drink?"

"I drink anything. And frequently. At the moment, I feel most regrettably sober. Probably the result of trauma." He watched her unlock an antique cocktail cabinet, the mahogany panels of which had not entirely been destroyed by playful wildlife, and pour the drinks. Big ones.

Looking at her, he decided that Camilla Greylaw was somewhat like the ancient sex goddess of the flicks—not so much in form, though there was enough of that to substantiate the claim, but more in manner. She had the same kind of impossible, wide-eyed, outrageous innocence—the childlike spirit imprisoned in a delicious instrument of orgasm. He liked her. It was quite possible that Fate or Kismet or that Great Computer in the Sky had rigged the rendezvous so that Camilla Greylaw and Gabriel Crome might together stamp a few wild footprints in the sand.

She gave him the drink.

"Yes, I will stay the night," said Gabriel. "It's already late enough for students and bounties to take more than a passing interest in a lone traveller, hopefully once more pissed. Book sculptors, incidentally, make sculpture from books. Logical, creative, even useful. Who reads books any more? They only take up space, collect dust and feed bugs."

"Students, yes. Bounty hunters, surely not. They have to wait till you're dead, don't they?"

"The more ambitious groups arrange matters for themselves . . . I think I would like another drink, please. Then you shall tell me what you said you should have told me. The drink may help me to believe it."

Camilla downed her own whisky and refilled the glasses. "Let's sit down," she said. "The cats make a mess of everything. But the settee is still sittable. They will have to go, of course. I can't live alone with a menagerie."

"The best place to begin," he suggested, "could be the beginning."

"That means Eustace. At least for this beginning. There were other beginnings, but they didn't involve cats and suicide."

"They will keep until this one ends. That reminds me—where did you get that five-kilo weight? It has been worrying me. I think we left it on the bridge."

"Eustace used it for weighing cat meat . . . It was quite romantic, I suppose. We met eighteen months ago in St.

James's Park when I was feeding the ducks and being attacked by a swarm of prepubes. I didn't realize they came out before sunset. But it was winter, and that might explain it."

"Did the little people want something special?"

"Just the usual. Money, jewellery, clothes. I don't think they really wanted to hurt me. The eldest was a terrifying child with two great scars on her cheeks, about ten years old."

"What did Eustace do—call the procs?"

"No, he dropped a gas egg. He always carried one or two with him. He was a very gentle person. He just couldn't stand violence . . . The gas hit us all, I think. When I woke up, I was here, still half undressed, and Eustace was watching Marilyn Monroe on the plate. I told you it did things to him. He saw I was awake, then he just looked at me and went mad." Camilla took another sip of whisky and laughed. "Poor Eustace! White hair, a Siggy Freud beard, striped trousers. He hadn't had a woman ever, I think. What a mess he made of it! I didn't know whether to mother him, show him how to do it or sit in the deep freeze. Afterwards, he spent practically all night crying and saying how sorry he was and how rich he was and conning me into a two-year marriage agreement."

Gabriel drank some more whisky to slow down his confusion. "And you married him because you felt sorry for him?"

"No, Gabriel. I married him because I felt sorry for myself. Before Eustace came along, I'd had a sort of drifting time. With men, I mean. Everybody seemed to want to bounce me, but nobody wanted to keep me. A lezzylove I used to sleep with when I was off the hot rod kick hit it right on the dildo. She said I was too intelligent and too stupid." Camilla also drank more whisky. "Too intelligent for the meat men and too stupid for the think tanks. I was the little doll they took to bed at night and put away in the morning. The trouble was, I could never afford a bed of my own."

This time it was Gabriel who poured the drinks. "I hope we are not more than half a bottle away from the pacifist tiger bit."

Camilla yawned. "Shouldn't think so. But there's a problem. I'm in the prommy phase, which is phase one, and whisky makes me more prommy, anyway. But you can't do it because of the dread disease."

"What disease?"

"V.D. Actually V.D. P 939, silly."

Gabriel felt dazed. Very dazed. It seemed long long ago since he had been innocently corrupting a raven at the Albert Memorial. He thought it high time he got a grip on reality. He thought it high time, also, that Camilla resolved various mysteries before too many others accrued. Eustace was a key word. So was marriage. He tried them.

"Eustace. Marriage."

"Yes, well, it was a two-year thing with five thousand on signature and five thousand on completion. Completion, by the way, is/was two or three months off. I told Eustace I wasn't going to renew." Camilla sighed. "Perhaps that's why he sliced himself on the Circle Line . . . I thought it was a reasonable offer, because ten thousand pounds will buy a fair amount of time and freedom and things, when you consider. Besides, I wasn't going to spend anything during the two years. Eustace had promised clothes, holidays, everything. He was a dear, really. I didn't even mind the Marilyn Monroe tapes and the fabulous fumblings. Left to his own devices, he could usually manage an orgasm after an hour or two. No, the one thing that really threw me was when he started turning the love nest into a refuge for bent animals."

"Where did he get them?"

"Coming, coming, coming to it," announced Camilla. She rolled her eyes. "Better not give me any more whisky, archangel mine, otherwise the wondrous tale will fizzle . . . Yes, he stole them. That's why top shriek—top secrecy. Do you know anything about mollycollybology?"

"Try again."

She tried. Hard. "Molly-cular-by-ology."

"Molecular biology. No. There was something about it, I think, on the buttock of my last reclining nude. But I didn't trouble to read."

"Ever the gentleman. Well, do you know anything about D.N.A.?"

"To surprise you, yes. It's a nucleic acid containing a sugar called deoxyribose. Further it lives—if one may flog the term—in the cell nucleus. Moreover, it is a double helix molecule which is the very stuff of life . . . I read that bit on the breast . . . D.N.A. Yes, I'm for it, on the whole."

"Don't confound me, Gabriel. Because I don't know anything at all about molecular biology, D.N.A., enzymes or anything else that goes bump in the lab. But Eustace did. In fact, when he wasn't getting hot about Marilyn Monroe and sweaty about me, he was away in his stunt house practising all sorts of perversions with bacteria, hard radiation, Petri dishes and God knows what other sex substitutes . . . But the message is as follows: he finally designed—he was fond of that word design—an interesting little creature called P 939. Its base model, he told me glowingly, was the bacterium that causes syphilis—a spirochete, I think he called it. But according to Eustace, P 939 was the best and latest venereal disease in the business. No really nasty effects. Except that if you caught it, you couldn't be beastly any more. I've changed my mind. I need another drink before I lose it all."

Gabriel poured some more whisky into each glass, and was

saddened to find that, as a result, the bottle was empty.

"What do you mean, you can't be beastly any more?"

"The aggressive instinct goes phut. P 939 inhibits aggression. You can't make war, you can't knock people about, you can hardly bear to upset them, even. That's what P 939 does to us. Fiendish, isn't it? When Eustace was sure he'd pulled it off, he thought he was Jesus Pasteur and Mahatma Einstein all rolled into one."

Gabriel drank some more whisky and looked at Camilla. He was in no shape to concentrate further on the saga of P 939. He was, however, able to decide that it would be a good and charitable act to offer Camilla Greylaw some consolation for her recent bereavement.

He kissed her. Camilla dropped her glass.

"It is all immensely interesting, but the rest of the story will keep. I fear I have an urgent engagement."

"Where?"

"In bed with you."

"The cats. You promised to help feed the cats."

"What will happen if we don't feed them till morning?"

"They'll cry. I couldn't bear them to cry. I suppose it's because I've got P 939 myself. And that's another reason why we shouldn't make love."

Gabriel sighed. "All right, the cats first. As for the dread disease, my dear mother at the Yurkuti Embassy used to say that a trouble shared is best shared in the most enjoyable way possible . . . Eustace had a limited imagination. You are more than Marilyn Monroe. You are Ayesha, Helen, Cleopatra, Elizabeth of Austria."

Camilla stood up, swaying a little. She felt weak at the knees, but it was a weakness not entirely due to the whisky. Gabriel held her close, remembering how he had held her on the bridge. Suddenly he was full of fierce possession. He had saved her from death and now she would repay with life. Big joke.

Camilla seemed to be shivering. "Let's deal with the cats quickly," she whispered. "Elizabeth of Austria is in season."

# CHAPTER FOUR

Lulu Tower, which stood where Buckingham Palace had been before the exigencies of economics and tourism caused it to be removed to Monarchiland in the Scottish Highlands, was the tallest building in London. Being a slender, domed cylinder exactly five hundred metres high, it was also one of the finest phallic symbols in Western Europe.

It was occupied in descending order by the most important institutions in the United Kingdom. The dome and the top fifty storeys housed NaTel, its governors, director-general, public relations officers, controllers, accountants, producers, telefamilies, camera crews, technicians, and make-up girls — even unto the lowly script spinners. Immediately under NaTel were the storeys that contained what was left of the Mother of Parliaments. And immediately beneath the two Parliament levels were the various ministries and government departments necessary to give the illusion of running a small country containing a mere seventy million people.

The branches of the Civil Service extended downwards for nearly one hundred storeys to the base of the building. At ground level, the Ministry of Education and the Ministry of Mental Health waged unending total war upon each other for possession of the greater number of eighty-eight small cell-like rooms. In fact both were fighting for a lost cause, since the Ministry of Sport was expanding downwards.

Occupying a south-facing room well above the critical half-way mark in the great glass and titanium phallus, Dr. Peregrine Perrywit found some cause for satisfaction. Few men had climbed the Thing from base to shining dome; but Dr. Perrywit, who had started with MinEd ten years ago, had now reached the seventy-seventh level. Not only that, but he was already on drinking terms with two NaTel producers (Get High With Mother and The Junior Sex Hour) and his wife had attracted the attention of a lush lezzy NaTel accountant. Dr. Perrywit, although still only in the mid-level of the Ministry of International Security and Race Harmony, was confident that he had far to go.

The possession of a B2 security pass carried with it certain advantages. He was, for example, able even now to shoot up to NaTel reception level without being challenged. He made it a practice to do so at least three times a week. Sometimes, he would walk out to one of the helicopter decks as if he had been assigned to meet an important incognito; and at other times he would take a drink in the guest bar, again with the air of one keeping a vital assignation.

But, as Dr. Perrywit sat at his desk and gazed through his double glazing on this fine summer morning, he was aware that before he could aspire to the giddy heights of NaTel, he needed to be at least two grades higher in Insect Race. And that would require talent and initiative. Both of which, naturally, he had in plenty.

Perhaps his chief talent was for the reduction of expenditure. Originally, he had specialized in divinity, gaining his Ph.D. in this skill. Divinity had been a necessary discipline because, in his youth, he had yearned to become a computer designer, specializing in the then new God Machines. It was a time of great opportunity. The Christian churches had integrated into Romaprot, which had hired the best business efficiency firm in the U.S.A. to switch the church to automation and restore the waning fortunes of religion to a sound commercial basis.

The computerization of God had caught not only the imagination of prollies and think tanks but also the imagination of Peregrine Perrywit, who was neither. The Instant Absolution advertising campaign (masterminded by the legendary Homer T. Krappe Associates) that followed the first phase of automation had started the folding money rolling in once more. Romaprot went public as a limited liability company and was oversubscribed instantly. Share values doubled, tripled, quadrupled. Peregrine Perrywit, hot from University and with the ink still wet on his Ph.D., had a thirty-five second interview with Cardinal Archbishop Cyril Cantuar and got hired on the spot.

To design God Machines.

Unfortunately, there was an almost immediate misunderstanding. Dr. Perrywit, of North Country origin and with a wired-in compulsion to thrift, was under the impression that he was to operate on a cost-efficiency basis. He was not. He was hired to spend money not to save it, Romaprot having reached that critical stage where it could no longer afford to think small.

Dr. Perrywit, after two years' intensive work, produced the design for a mobile, confession-hearing, advice-proffering, absolution-dispensing, French/English/German/Italian-speaking God Machine that could be manufactured for less than nine hundred thousand pounds.

He was fired. Not only as project-leader but from Romaprot employment altogether.

His rival project-leader had had the wit to produce a machine that could do all that Dr. Perrywit's machine could do. Further, it could play the organ, produce plainsong, conduct baptism, confirmation, expulsion, marriage, divorce, euthanasia and death ceremonies while simultaneously playing a useful part in Romaprot's vast accounting procedures. The fact that it would cost five million to build was an additional argument in its favour.

So Dr. Perrywit was consigned to the limbo of MinEd. His thrift compulsion went with him. He succeeded in cutting the budget of his first project—the computerized control of nappy changing in State crèches—by twenty per cent. MinEd saw the writing on the wall and shot him upstairs.

MinSport suffered a similar ordeal by Perrywit when he attempted to introduce plastic grass in two thousand football stadia throughout the country. The saving would have amounted to more than twenty million pounds a year. Perrywit was clearly dangerous, so again they shot him upstairs.

Insect Race, however, knew how to make use of Dr. Perrywit's peculiar talent. As the largest and most expensive ministry in the Thing, Insect Race swallowed one quarter of the nation's annual income. And at times it had come dangerously near to spending one third. It needed Dr. Perrywit. It needed him badly. The Ministry of International Security and Race Harmony was basically responsible for the armed forces, the diplomatic service, foreign aid, scientific research and the maintenance and organization of an *élite* cadre of agents provocateurs.

At present, Dr. Perrywit's talent was devoted to scientific research. And for the past few weeks he had been concentrating on decimation of the Microbiological Warfare Division with a target of reducing its overall budget by fifty per cent.

That is why he had fired Professor Eustace Greylaw after forty years of almost blameless and even, on occasion, almost meritorious service. That is also why he was concerned with the problem of disposing of various animals, while at the same time ascertaining what had happened to one tiger, one squirrel, one lion, one lamb, one panther and one white rabbit.

Ten years before, Professor Greylaw had received an important brief from the then Chief of MicroWar (since elevated to anchor man for NaTel's Beauties of Mother Nature series). Professor Greylaw had been instructed to develop a micro-organism that could be used over a period of time to ease any aggressive nation out of its war psychology without it looking as if there had been external interference. This was a tall, if not impossible, order. Which is why O.C. MicroWar had chosen Professor Greylaw.

Throughout his generally undistinguished career, Eustace Greylaw had been accident prone. Ask him to develop a new Black Death, and the chances were he would have absent-mindedly wiped out the Home Counties before he had finished proving the bug. Ask him to develop a form of instant trypanosomiasis suitable for use in a cold climate and he would have put half Scandinavia to sleep before he was satisfied that he had accomplished the task.

Professor Greylaw was dedicated, conscientious and pains-taking—which is to say dangerous. So he had been given an impossible task simply to keep him out of trouble. Eustace Greylaw still had enough grip on the external world to realize why he had been removed from the plum project of irreversible brain damage and consigned to the limbo of anti-aggression. So, determined to spite everyone by achieving the impossible, he had conducted his work in grim secrecy. Apart from the fact that he used up a lot of animals, no one knew what progress he was making. After a time, when O.C. MicroWar was promoted to NaTel's Uncle Dan, nobody even knew what he was supposed to be doing. Naturally, he neglected to inform anyone of his success. Naturally, after Dr. Perrywit had discovered that, over the last nine years, Professor Greylaw's annual budget had averaged ninety thousand pounds, Eustace was fired.

The only remaining problems, as far as Dr. Perrywit was concerned, were how to account for the loss of various animals and how to dispose of the occupants of what was left of the Greylaw zoo, a ramshackle collection of huts and cages which, until the Perrywit era, had enjoyed a maximum security rating.

He had an idea. He pressed the toe stud under his desk.

In imagination, he saw a tall busty blonde goddess in a white cat-suit enter his office. He sprang round the desk and locked the door, secure in the knowledge that the office was completely soundproofed. The goddess whirled with a look of alarm on her face. But he was too quick for her. He leaped towards her, whipping the freezair pencil from his pocket.

One brief squirt and the goddess froze. He lowered her rigid body gently to the carpet. Then he gave her the merest whiff of relaxant, so that her muscles slackened, though she still could not move.

Her eyes were open and she had to look at him. Yes, that was good. She had to look at him. He kissed her savagely. He bit her lips, her ears, her neck. He crushed beautifully inert mountains of female tissue in his cruel fingers. He tore at the cat-suit, flinging himself upon her in an ecstasy of brutal frenzy. How the strength was upon him! He thrust savagely—once, twice, three times. Always she had to look. Was that a moan? Please let her be relaxed enough to be able to moan!

The only question left was should he strangle her at the

36

point of orgasm . . .

His daydream was shattered as the door opened and a tall busty goddess in a white cat-suit entered his office.

"Good morning, Dr. Perrywit."

"Ah, good morning, Dr.—ah—Slink." He wiped the sweat from his forehead and tried to control his breathing. Heart still racing. That was bad. He opened a drawer and fumbled for the tiny pink pills.

"Was there something, sir?"

"Yes—yes, there was." He found the pills and swallowed one. "The Greylaw matter. I delegated it to you. All satisfactory? He—ah—he took it well?"

"I never actually saw Professor Greylaw. I don't think anybody now here has actually seen him. Though I'm told he did attend a seventieth level conference eighteen years ago . . . I think there is something you ought to know, Dr. Perrywit. A few days after his retirement, the Professor died rather sadly."

"How?"

"He—he fell under a Circle Line train."

There was a moment's silence, then Dr. Perrywit—still disconcerted by recent non-events—briefly lost control. "Bastard!" he shrieked. "Lazy, deceitful bastard! Why couldn't he have done it ten days ago and saved us that massive severance fee?"

Dr. Slink looked at him, shocked. One of these days he really would squirt her and savage that proud voluptuous body; and she would have to look at him while he was doing it, and . . .

With an effort Dr. Perrywit shook himself out of it. "I didn't mean it that way, Dorothea. But, responsible as I am for MicroWar's money—oh, hell, what are we going to do about the animals, the ones that are left? At least we can lose the feed bill."

"We could have them put down, Dr. Perrywit. It is standard procedure for MicroWar experimental animals on project termination."

"Waste! Think of the waste. Squirrels, yes, but cats are worth a lot these days . . . Experimental animals indeed! What did Greylaw do? No records, no anything. No project specification even. Only the code-name Tranquillity. The old footler just fed his pussies for nine years at the expense of MicroWar, Insect Race and the great British Public . . . Last time I saw the inventory there were elephants. What happened to them?"

"One broke out and got killed."

"How?"

"It derailed the London-Brighton hovertrain. The other one died of a broken heart."

"Hm. We really will have to trace those missing cats. The records you know. I need my records absolutely perfect."

"Yes, Dr. Perrywit."

"Perfection, symmetry, balance, order, economy—these, Dr. Slink, are vanishing ideals in an age of chaos. But while I live I will strive to attain . . ." He was suddenly struck by a brilliant thought. "You needn't worry about the surviving animals, I think I have a solution, an elegant solution. Meanwhile, see they get enough to eat. They are your responsibility."

"Yes, Dr. Perrywit. Thank you." She turned to go.

"Oh, and Dr. Slink."

She half turned back. Those proud and living mountains stared disdainfully at him with their hidden X-ray eyes of nipples.

"You look," he croaked, "you look, you look very—ah—efficient this morning."

"Thank you, Dr. Perrywit." Her nostrils quivered, an eyebrow ascended one point five millimetres, then she turned and opened the door. She closed it quietly behind her.

Dr. Perrywit took another pill. Then he began to contemplate his elegant solution.

Upon succeeding, the Marquis of Middlehampton had been saddled with death duties of about three mill. So he had sensibly turned Middle Acres into a combined tourist centre and nature reserve. What would he not say to the magnificent no-strings-attached gift of three big cats?

And the younger brother of the Marquis was no less than the Games, Contests and Prize Programmes Controller of NaTel. The only question was: could one—in these days of crumbling values—rely upon the noblesse to oblige?

## CHAPTER FIVE

The bed looked like a battlefield—as, in some respects, it had been. Gabriel, naked, lay back against the pillow with a smile of satisfaction on his lips and dark rings of exhaustion round his eyes. Camilla had not overstated when she claimed to be in the promiscuous phase. The last couple of times he had not been able to make it—which was annoying, because he had wanted to.

Camilla, also naked, rested her chin on her hands and gazed through the window at tree-tops in the late morning sunlight. The energy of the child was astounding. Almost at dawn, when Gabriel was thinking sorrowfully in terms of knock-out drops and/or a blood transfusion, she had risen from the bed of frenzy to round up the animals which had been enjoying a brief interval of discreet freedom in the garden. She had locked them in the cellar, turned the auto-vac loose on the ground floor, made a life-saving pot of tea, and had then given herself and Gabriel their badly needed anti-hangover shots.

After that, there was more ecstasy. Now, Gabriel was utterly limp; but Camilla still looked fresh enough for another round or two. Fortunately, P 939 prevented her from being aggressive about it.

"I think I shall ask a God Machine," she said.

Gabriel, whose thoughts—such as they were—had been in various elsewheres, looked at her in bewilderment. "A God Machine? What were we talking about?"

"We weren't. I was thinking."

"Then what were you thinking about?"

"P 939. Eustace. Us. The world. People. Responsibility. But mostly P 939."

"Ah, yes. P 939."

She grinned. "It's a stone cold, cast iron, twenty-four carat certainty that you have it now, darling . . . And then there were two."

He frowned, shook his head, then smiled. "Yes, then there were two. You got it from Eustace, I suppose?"

"Not in that sense. Actually," she giggled, "I received it by injection."

"Is it exactly the same bug the animals have?"

"No, but a close relation. Eustace tailored a breed specially for humans."

"I see." Gabriel was silent for a while. "These MicroWar people that Eustace worked for—surely they know all about it."

"No."

"Why?"

"Eustace wouldn't tell them. Palace politics, and all that excreta. Eustace said they'd given him an impossible project as a way of getting him out of the way. So, his sense of humour being what it was, he made a success of the project and wouldn't tell anybody. He took himself off to the Sussex downs, got his little zoo and lab organized and—as far as MicroWar was concerned—he went into retreat."

"I like your Eustace."

"So did I. Sometimes."

Gabriel thought for a while. He was very tired. Thinking was an effort. Eventually, he arrived at the obvious conclusion. "So it amounts to this: Eustace cooked it, you and I have it, and nobody else knows."

"Sweetie, that is the state of play. Hence the God Machine. This thing is bigger than both of us."

Gabriel pulled a face. "I wish my promiscuous phase was coming faster. What happens after that?"

"Eustace didn't prove it with humans. That is what makes me think the Circle Line gambit was a bit odd. Surely, when he had shot me full of the bug, curiosity would have kept him alive . . . With lions and suchlike, the prommy phase lasts about ten days. Then comes phase two—compulsive eating. That lasts about a month. After that, hypersensitivity and splendid tranquillity." She kissed him severally. "I hope you don't regret the night's work, darling. Eustace didn't say if it was a good thing for book sculpture."

Gabriel did his best to ignore the kisses. "Are you religious, Camilla?"

"I don't know. It isn't something I have ever really paused to consider."

"Then why the God Machine?"

"Well, one can't just consult people, can one? An opinion survey wouldn't work." She giggled. "Scusa, madam. I represent a new venereal disease which inhibits aggression, and I would be very glad to have your reaction . . . No, Gabriel. Talk to a stranger about something like this, and pretty soon the procs waft you away on air. Then the grill—T-bone special. Then MicroWar; and in the end Insect Race will probably put you away for life."

Gabriel considered the prospect gloomily. "I have a friend who says the God Machines are rigged."

"Rigged for what?"

"Rigged to provide information to interested parties. Romaprot is the largest industrial concern in the western world. It has more data about more people than all the intelligence networks put together. Wouldn't it be reasonable to sell information that was useful?"

Camilla smiled. "You are forgetting one thing. Millions and millions of people use the God Machines. It would take a vast army just to plough through all those boring secrets. And then it would take thousands of experts to decide what was useful and what wasn't . . . No, Gabriel, it couldn't be done."

"It could—by computer."

She was silent for a moment or two. Then she shook her head. "Not on. Too dangerous. Romaprot's prosperity is founded on the idea of complete privacy and complete impartiality. People trust the God Machines. After all, that is how it is supposed to be between us and God. If Romaprot lost that selling point, nobody would ever go to confession, would they?"

"I still don't think we should say anything about P 939 to a God Machine."

"Darling, they are only computers linked to other computers."

"Then why consult one?"

"Because they know a lot more than we do. Because if you feed them the data, they can predict results that would never occur to us . . . Do you know if P 939 is basically a good thing or a bad thing?"

"No."

"Neither do I. But a God Machine will. And then it will

43

tell us what to do about the bug."

"Let's compromise. If you insist on consulting a God Machine, don't give it any information by which we could be traced. Don't mention MicroWar or research or anything. Just ask it general questions, like what would happen if there was a contagious disease that knocked out aggression."

"All right, we'll do it that way. Satisfied?"

"I suppose so . . . I wish I could think more clearly."

"Don't. There really isn't any hurry about anything." Camilla yawned and stretched. Then she turned towards Gabriel and began to caress his shoulders. Then she wriggled until she lay on top of him and began to nibble his ear.

Gabriel noted his own reaction with amazement and alarm. "Why don't we calm down a little and go and have a bath?" he suggested without much hope.

# CHAPTER SIX

The brothers Karamazov, being identical twins, were unique
in the spy business. Nobody knew they were identical twins.
Nobody, in fact, knew that there was more than one Karamazov. Being economical though at the same time liking the
good things in life, they shared a single room at the Dorchester Hotel during their London jaunt.

The room had been taken in the name of Peter Ilyich
Karamazov. Sometimes letters arrived for Mr. Peter Karamazov as well as Mr. Ilyich Karamazov; but since the
Dorchester knew of only one Karamazov, all such mail found
its way into pigeon-hole 504 and thus, eventually, to room
504. The settee was quite as comfortable as the bed; but,
democratically, the brothers took turns.

Their uniqueness in the field of intelligence had been
assured some thirty years before when their father, Alexander,
and their mother, Tanya, had divorced in Paris. Alexander

45

went to the U.S.A. with Peter and Tanya went to the U.S.S.R. with Ilyich.

Both father and mother, who had been small-time agents —chiefly unsuccessful—and who had lived dangerously less because of counter-intelligence activities than because of malnutrition, worked hard at the Master Plan.

The Master Plan had been Alexander's—generated, no doubt, by the frequent application of cheap brandy to an empty stomach. If young Peter and young Ilyich could be groomed for future subversive stardom in, respectively, Washington and Moscow, the old age of their parents would be exceedingly bright.

Oddly, the plan worked up to a point. Peter, as a Russian-speaking, naturalized American with a good grasp of politics, was recruited by a blank-faced anonymous employee of the Committee for International Understanding almost before he had forged the seal and signature on his Master's Degree in Creative Brainwashing. Ilyich, as an American-speaking Russian, a member of the Karl Marx Mental Health League and a young man who had demonstrated outstanding loyalty by denouncing the political instability of his mother, was accepted for training by the Socialists for Inspirational Undertakings.

Although Ilyich had arranged for mother to be phased out in Siberia while Peter financed father on a crash-course in degenerative alcoholism in New York, the Master Plan proceeded with only slight modification.

Eventually, Cominunder was overjoyed to have it proved beyond doubt that agent Peter Karamazov had actually penetrated Russian intelligence at a high level. Socinunder was similarly filled with ecstasy to have a star operative demonstrate that he had access to the very fastnesses of Cominunder. In practice, Peter and Ilyich had simply rendezvoused in Geneva for a pleasant fortnight's holiday concluded only by a sordid half-hour of business. Peter had swapped the British irreversible brain-damage project for the French death-rain project contributed by Ilyich. Together, they then opened a Swiss numbered account into which they deposited half their respective bonuses.

From this modest beginning, they worked up to heights of artistic brilliance. It was their aim to amass ten million new Swiss Francs in ten years and then retire. Peter's ultimate ambition was to buy a small Pacific island and found a nudist free-love colony based on communal parenthood and the renunciation of personal possessions. Ilyich simply wanted to be the first Russian Governor of California. In order to make both projects possible they needed only to acquire ten million new Swiss Francs and then to change names.

At the present point in history, they had less than three years and four million Francs to go. Until now they had had perfect trust in each other and had worked in perfect harmony. Indeed, on occasion, each had helped the other out. Was it not Ilyich who had saved the U.S. President from assassination in Morocco when Peter had been grounded by dysentery? And was it not Peter who had smuggled the Soviet Ambassador out of Washington when he had flipped his lid and tried to defect?

But now, there was just the merest germ of suspicion and resentment between them—brought about, somewhat inadvertently, by the late Professor Eustace Greylaw.

It had been Ilyich who had suggested the holiday in England. No serious business this time, unless you could count the exchange of the Israeli anti-robot system for the United Arab Republic's robot guerilla. The brothers would simply relax, take in a few shows and diversions and talk of old times.

Unfortunately, one sunny afternoon, shortly after the

retirement of Professor Greylaw, Ilyich was strolling in St. James's Park when he met Dr. Slink of MicroWar. She was sitting on a bench, crying. She was also under the illusion that Ilyich was Peter, who had semi-seduced her in a sort of spiritual fashion some months previously for the MicroWar budget estimates.

She was crying because Dr. Perrywit had been bullying her about her arithmetic, because he had also taken to looking at her in rather strange ways, because she hadn't realized how much money Professor Greylaw had spent without accounting for it, because life in MicroWar was less romantic than she had formerly supposed, and because Dr. Perrywit still seemed to hold her personally responsible for various missing animals. She was also crying because it was a wonderful day and she wanted to dance naked on the grass, surrounded by bronzed young men who would adore without actually touching.

"Peter!" she sobbed. "Peter! How utterly nice to see you. Come and cheer me up." She knew, of course, that Peter Karamazov worked for Cominunder; but that didn't matter, really, because after all we were all on the same side. And, anyway, he was a gentleman.

Ilyich froze momentarily, then became Peter and managed a warm smile of recognition. This sort of thing had happened before.

"Forgive me," he said. "I almost passed you. This is one of my difficult days. There was some trouble recently in Cairo . . . The medicos said I would get odd recurring patches of amnesia. Your face—I could not forget that, but . . ." he passed his hand over his forehead and sat down on the bench.

"Poor Peter. Poor dear Peter. I'm Dorothea, remember? Dorothea Slink. Insect Race. MicroWar." She dabbed at her eyes and gazed modestly at the ground. "We—we worked together last winter."

Insect Race. MicroWar. Gone for Ilyich was the holiday atmosphere. He was the professional once more.

"Dorothea, of course! I told you it was only brief. How are you? Why are you crying? You shall tell me all about it."

Presently, with some sympathetic but entirely spiritual encouragement (Ilyich had quite as much intuitive knowledge of women as Peter), Dr. Slink was pouring out her heart about Dr. Perrywit, Professor Greylaw, the outrageous budget and the missing animals. She also confided to Ilyich/Peter that she had several times tried to contact Professor Greylaw at his Sussex zoo; but the Professor had always been so elusive. She had tried his home once, but to no avail. In the end, she had had to fire him *in absentia*. And, really, nothing seemed to have ever happened at the zoo. No research, no anything. The animals were very pleasant, though, extremely friendly and docile. You could even stroke the big ones; and there was a rabbit actually playing with a tiger. No wonder the code-name was Tranquillity. Really, it looked as if that silly Professor had just been playing some elaborate and silly joke . . .

Ilyich listened carefully to Dr. Slink's recital; and when the narrative waned a little, he prompted her with pertinent questions. After ten minutes he was convinced that Dr. Slink knew no more of this mysterious affair than she had already told him. He was also convinced that he was on to something interesting. That sixth Karamazov sense made a discreet noise in his head like bundles of folding money falling on to a desk.

He tried to look pale and wan, made vague references to an appointment with his psychiatrist and so far forgot himself, or rather Peter, as to kiss Dr. Slink's hand in florid continental style.

For a moment, he nervously fingered the ice-needle gun in

his pocket; but fortunately the woman had not noticed his gaffe.

"You will call me, Peter, won't you? It is so nice to have someone *simpatico* to talk to." She lowered her eyes. "I still live alone, you know, and I do not care much for social vulgarities. Essentially, I suppose, I am a home bird."

"My dear—my dearest Dorothea," Ilyich judged that she would relish the implied intimacy, "I shall not only call you, I shall haunt you. But first I must see my psychiatrist and then I shall need a day or two to clear up some trifling assignment."

"I understand. It is terribly, terribly top secret, I suppose?"

"Terribly. But I can tell you this: MicroWar will appreciate the result. Hands across the drink. That kind of thing. Say nothing to anyone. There are dangers."

"I understand. *Au 'voir.*"

"*'Wiedersehen.*"

Having escaped from Dr. Slink, Ilyich wasted no time. It took him only half an hour to locate Professor Greylaw's private residence and rent a fifteenth floor one-room apartment with uninterrupted view less than one kilometre from 1735, Babscastle Boulevard. There he set up a 50 x 50 telescope and peered down over the high wall that surrounded the Professor's garden. At dusk he saw a rabbit chasing a lion on the lawn. Later, he raised the telescope slightly to enjoy Camilla undressing for a bath. Eustace Greylaw was also enjoying the same view, but from close up. There appeared to be some mild sexual interplay, then Eustace fell into the bath. Presently, the lights went off. Ilyich felt frustrated and returned to the Dorchester.

Peter was already in their room. Ilyich did not tell Peter about Dr. Slink or Professor Greylaw. It was a tactical error.

The following day, with a beautiful plastic white-carnation directional microphone in his lapel, Ilyich rose early and stalked the Professor. Peter, himself blessed with that sixth Karamazov sense, also rose early and stalked Ilyich. The three of them went by hovertrain to Bognor Regis. Then they all went by separate autocabs to the zoo.

It was in a tiny remote valley and was surrounded by a high wire fence and the usual Insect Race No Entry to Unauthorized Personnel advertisements. The Professor unlocked the gate, then locked it again behind him.

Ilyich did not try to enter. Neither did Peter. The Professor disappeared into one of the huts. Then he came out and went into another hut. There were vague animal noises from various small compounds. Presently, the Professor began to feed his pets.

It was while Eustace was fondling a lion that Ilyich realized the Professor was also talking to the creature. One never knew.

Ilyich aimed the directional carnation, estimated range, adjusted volume and put the plug in his ear.

His head rattled with the thunderous sound of the lion purring. He adjusted the volume control and consequently lost what the Professor was saying. Presently, he caught something of the rhythm of the operation and managed to get snatches of professional soliloquy without suffering too greatly.

What he heard convinced him that he was not wasting his time.

"We'll show them, won't we, pussy cat? PURR PURR. We'll show them that Eustace Greylaw is a PURR PURR to be reckoned with. We'll PURR PURR the greatest synthetic disease in the PURR PURR until every man, woman and beast is PURR PURR SHLURDASHERVEROO-VEROO!"

The lion had sneezed.

Ilyich tore the plug from his ear—too late. The train in

pain stayed mainly in his brain until it finally disappeared down a long tunnel of de-escalating anguish. His hands trembled. Sweat formed on his forehead.

The Professor was still talking to pussy cat; but the Karamazov courage was no longer equal to the Karamazov curiosity.

Eventually, Professor Greylaw, having concluded his speech to the lion, seemed also to have concluded his business at the zoo. Presently three autocabs—discreetly spaced—returned to Bognor Regis.

Professor Greylaw, followed by Ilyich followed by Peter, then took the next hovertrain back to London Victoria.

It was while the Professor was standing near the edge of the platform at Victoria tube station, waiting for a Circle Line train, that he began to talk once more. To himself, this time, since there were no lions present and, apart from the brothers Karamazov, no one else seemed to be interested in what he was saying.

Ilyich had recovered his nerve sufficiently to try the white-carnation microphone once more. But there were others present on the platform, and several people passed between him and the Professor.

"So I said to this student (a girl's voice) if you put it in like that again, I'll . . . and then we used the freezair (a male prepube) and then we rolled this granny down the steps and then . . ."

It was hopeless. Ilyich took the plug out of his ear.

He decided to take a chance. He edged his way closer and closer to Professor Greylaw, while looking casually in the opposite direction. It was just as he reached the Professor's side that he saw Peter momentarily and carelessly raise his head above the top of a colour tri-di girliezine. Ilyich stumbled slightly with surprise. He put out his hand to steady himself. The hand touched the Professor's shoulder.

The Professor stopped muttering to himself and turned round.

If there was one thing in life that Eustace Greylaw hated, it was plastic flowers. It went back to childhood. Mummy had always liked lots of gay plastic flowers in her gay suburban home. Daddy had shot her. Eustace had gone to a State Retreat for Maladjusted Prepubes.

Professor Greylaw and Ilyich Karamazov confronted each other. Briefly.

The Professor registered a vaguely unlikeable face and a quite terrifying button hole. Appalled, he stepped back. The train came in.

Professor Greylaw's lips were moving even as he fell off the platform.

Ilyich tried desperately to lip read. He failed.

It would not have informed him greatly if he had succeeded.

Eustace Greylaw's last words were: "My God! A plastic carnation!"

Ilyich faded into the crowd. Peter faded into the crowd. They met outside the station, found the nearest Dial-'n'-Drink and ordered large Japanese whiskies.

"Why did you kill him, brother?"

"I didn't kill him. Why did you follow me, brother?"

"I didn't follow you."

"Liar!"

"Liar!"

"Peter?"

"Ilyich?"

"You must believe me. I didn't kill him."

"You must believe *me*. I didn't follow you. But I know that you have something, and you are not sharing it."

"It was too early. I intended to share it. I will share it now."

53

"Good. Then all will be as it was before. Brothers and comrades, Ilyich." Peter raised his glass.

"Yes, brothers and comrades, Peter." Ilyich raised his glass. "All will be as it was before."

But even when he had told everything he knew, all was not as it was before. Something fine had gone out of their lives.

"And he said nothing to you when he fell?"

"Nothing, brother."

"I saw his lips move."

"So did I. But I heard nothing."

Peter Karamazov sighed. One Swiss numbered account was no longer enough. Presently, there would have to be two.

# CHAPTER SEVEN

Although St. Paul's Cathedral was dwarfed somewhat by the forty-storey Winston Churchill Retreat for Alcoholics and the fifty-storey Bertrand Russell Twilight Tower (Voluntary Euthanasia Ltd.), its dome still retained the proud patina and bird droppings of time, the dignity and flaked masonry of the centuries. Since Romaprot had put the guts back into religion—on a sound seven-per-cent annual growth basis—there had been changes. Inevitable changes. But they had been carried out tastefully, with foresight, and as good investments.

The choir and high altar had had to go, naturally, to make way for a fragment of Comptroller's Department and Computer Engineering Division; but Sir James Thornhill's paintings still retained their lofty eminence, and there were plastic replicas of original Grinling Gibbons carvings adorning the discreetly styled executive cells.

In the centre of the nave a perpetual fountain of irridescent holy water gave movement and vitality to the very heart of the cathedral. The mineralogical content of the water met the exact specifications of the spring at Lourdes; and in the extended crypt one thousand bathing cubicles were available on a ten-minute or twenty-minute rental basis. On either side of the nave were the ranks of auto-confession booths, wired up to four God Machines appropriately located in the Whispering Gallery, and programmed to accept all major currencies. Due to the recent invention of Depthorama, the booths were also equipped to supply Instant Full Cathedral Services in American, Russian, Europarl, Afritawk and Chinese and (also by dial selection) in modern Romaprot style as well as ancient Greek Orthodox, Anglican and Catholic. The services were divided into First Class, Economy Class and Mini-shot, according to the means and time available to the worshipper. For ten pounds, up to six people could be uplifted for two hours by Depthorama recordings of Cardinal Archbishop Cyril Cantuar, the NaTel Black and White Choir, and musical dramatization of a choice of parables, miracles and assorted preachings—all shot on location with authorized Equity actors and nudes. With Nativity, Crucifixion and Resurrection, all seasonably popular items, there was a ten per cent surcharge.

Outside the cathedral, Romaprot had provided for the requirements of all intending worshippers. Cathedral Reception surrounded the ancient building like a vast steel and hiduminium torus. It contained a subterranean coffee-bar in the form of a creatively improved replica of a torture-chamber of the Spanish Inquisition; a compact Sistine Chapel restaurant; and the Holy Sepulchre intimate all-nite-spot for late and early visitors.

Ripple sky signs fixed on top of Cathedral Reception proclaimed simple exhortations, moving and self-evident truths:

God Can Process You; Give Him the Data and Pick Up the Output; He Keeps You in His Memory Banks; You Too Will Come Clean in that Great Detergent in the Sky; God is Feedback; He has Computer Time For All.

It was already dusk when Camilla and Gabriel arrived at Reception. It was a busy time of day, since many students, prollies, prepubes and even procs and bounty hunters preferred to confess before the night's work had really started, and the traffic board indicated a twenty-minute wait for booths. Camilla went to the rentals counter and paid for ten minutes advice/confession time for two. She received a numbered metal tab, upon which was stamped the date and time of application and the amount and classification of computer time paid for, then she and Gabriel went to take Irish coffee at the Spanish Inquisition.

Surprisingly, they managed to get a table to themselves. Gabriel was in a sombre mood, partly because he disapproved of confiding in a God Machine and partly because he was very very tired.

He sipped his coffee silently for a while then glanced at the wall score plate. It was changing numbers fairly rapidly, and was at present flipping through the eight thousand one hundreds.

"What number have we got?"

Camilla looked at the tab. "Eight thousand nine hundred and seven."

"Not more than about ten minutes, I suppose. Unless a number of prosperous citizens can suddenly afford a lot of computer time . . . Don't forget the deal, Camilla. False names. False everything."

"False everything," she agreed, smiling. "You are too cautious, Gabriel. I think I love you."

"I love you, too . . . Suppose it tells us to go and confess all to Insect Race?"

"Then it will give us reasons. We may be dangerous people, hazards to society, and all that. After all, unless we remain faithful to each other . . ."

"I'd like to be a hazard to society," said Gabriel with some feeling. "By the way, did Eustace ever say anything about antidotes, cures, that sort of thing?"

"He seemed fairly confident about the resistance of P 939. I think he was of the opinion that it would be a fairly hard beast to hammer . . . I suppose it also helps that no one yet knows of its existence."

"They will," said Gabriel gloomily. "They will."

"Anyway, it doesn't matter, really. We haven't committed any crime."

"Eustace has, and you and I are his accomplices. We are receivers of stolen bacteria. P 939 belongs to MicroWar. So do the animals that Eustace also stole."

"Ah, yes. The animals. We will have to do something about them. Quite apart from being MicroWar property, they are exhausting to live with."

Camilla glanced at the score plate and saw that her tab number would shortly come up.

"Finish your coffee. It's almost time for Divine Guidance. If we miss our number, they can charge waiting time."

They went to the cathedral's main entrance, received a benign smile from the computer-controlled priest-automaton on duty, inserted the metal tab in the assignment slot and waited a moment while a God Machine told the priest which booth to send them to.

The priest-automaton had evidently been programmed to speak with an Irish accent. "Sure and it's a foin avenin' for liftin' the weight from your souls, me darlin's. His Eminence will receive you in B 27. First left, second right, and go with God."

The booth itself was totally enclosed, air-conditioned and

tastefully furnished. Inside, six contour chairs faced the Depthorama screen that gave the occupants of the confession booth the illusion of being entirely alone in a vast uncluttered replica of the cathedral. As Camilla and Gabriel each sat in a contour chair, the light dimmed, the scent of summer woodland filled the air and there was the piped rustling of leaves in a light breeze. The Depthorama vision of the cathedral dissolved into a magnificent sunset.

There was a great cloud, fleeced in fire. Standing on the cloud, clothed in a robe of radiance and majesty, was a dramatic El Greco type figure. It seemed very far away and at the same time strangely near. Underneath the cloud, in violet letters etched into the sunset, were the words: *Deus ex Machina.*

Divinity spoke—in excellent middle middle-class English, the words echoing as if through long corridors of space and time.

"Greetings, my children," said Divinity. "Give me your burdens and be at peace."

J.S. Bach made a brief contribution to proceedings with a piped forty-five second clip from Toccata and Fugue in D.

Divinity became a shade more informal: "My children, it is fitting that we should know each other fully, that your troubles should be consigned to the great memory banks of eternity. Namepads, please."

"Marilyn Monroe," said Camilla. "I live in Union Tower, Highgate."

"Michael Angelo," said Gabriel. "Barbican Seventeen."

"Marilyn and Michael," said Divinity softly. "Know that I hold you close. Which of you will speak to me first?"

"I will, Father," said Camilla.

"Proceed, my daughter. Speak now of what is close to your heart."

"Well, Father," began Camilla, "the problem is not really ours. It concerns a friend of ours. He thinks he has invented a contagious disease that will stop people wanting to hurt or kill each other. He wants to know what to do."

"Child, this friend of yours should be with us now. Where is he?"

"He will not come, Father. He has not seen the light."

Divinity sighed. "Alas, for those who have eyes and cannot see. Alas for those who choose to walk in darkness . . . What, then, is his namepad?"

"Father, I cannot say. He asked us not to reveal it."

Divinity was saddened. "Daughter, there should be no secrets between us . . . Is your friend a scientist?"

"Yes, Father."

"Is the disease transmitted by micro-organisms?"

"Yes, Father."

"Has your friend proved his disease upon living creatures?"

"Yes, Father."

Divinity changed position on his cloud, adopting a gently stern attitude.

"My daughter, your friend is in a state of mortal sin — unless his work has been sanctioned by authorized representatives of government and/or a responsible industrial research programme."

Gabriel decided to speak. "Our friend works only for his own interest. He simply wishes to know if it would be a good thing if men were unable to make war any more."

"Disease is the scourge of God," said Divinity severely. "Men shall not take it upon themselves to interfere with the laws of Nature—unless invested with the proper authority. It—" Divinity paused, then Depthorama zoomed him down from the cloud for a frowning close-up. "My children, you yourselves have sinned greatly. Marilyn Monroe does not live in Union Tower, Highgate. There is no Union Tower, Highgate. Michael Angelo does not live in Barbican Seventeen . . . If you are not ill or high, my children, there can only be mischief in your hearts. Here in the House of God you are free to speak fully at all times. You are even free to withhold the truth. Such is the quality of infinite mercy . . . However, if you have faith, I recommend you to rest tranquilly while I summon priests of the Psychiatric and Social Order who will help—"

Gabriel did not wait for the rest. He jumped out of his contour seat as if stung. He groped for the master-switch and brought light back into the auto-confession booth. The Depthorama faded. It seemed highly probable that the P.S.O. priests were already on their way.

"Gabriel, what—"

"No time. Quick." He grabbed Camilla's hand and pulled her to the door. It seemed to be jammed.

Cursing dreadfully to himself, Gabriel darted to the master control console and pressed every button he could find. He ordered Greek Orthodox, Anglican and Catholic services, First Class, in Russian, Europarl and Afritawk. He ordered the Black and White Choir, three miracles and the Crucifixion.

Still cursing, and blessed apparently with superhuman strength, he tore the console from the wall and hurled it at the Depthorama screen. And then he found what he had been looking for all the time—the red emergency exit and fire button installed under Romaprot Fire Regulation 92B. He hit it.

The door opened automatically, heavy rain seemed to be coming from somewhere, and a circular section of the ceiling fell in. From the direction of the Depthorama screen, a high-speed voice gabbled: "Go forth and multiply! Go forth and multiply! Go forth and multiply."

Gabriel and Camilla fled.

# CHAPTER EIGHT

Dr. Slink was alone with her secret persona in her twenty-fifth storey apartment in Margot Fonteyn House, Shepherd's Bush. The apartment was lushly feminine with frills and fripperies all over the place. In fact, it was not so much an apartment as a boudoir of the soul. She had a plastic reproduction four-poster bed on which she hoped—one day—to be ravished by a prince, or at least a high-echelon executive of NaTel. She had a Persian carpet, a tiger-skin and a goat-skin rug. She had *Blindman's Buff* by Fragonard over the mantel-piece and *Napoleon in his Study* by David in the bathroom. Sometimes when she was bathing and looked at Napoleon, she trembled a little. Perhaps there was just a hint of Dr. Perrywit in that penetrating gaze . . .

It was evening, and the door was electro-locked and the student alarms were set and the freezair pencil was by her bed, and Dr. Slink had abandoned herself to the strange whims of that disguised hamadryad, Dorothea.

She was sitting naked on the goat-skin rug, eating chocolate creams and listening to taped Strauss waltzes. She was in heaven. She was also in a Ruritanian day-dream of considerable poignancy. There were tears in her eyes but she bravely held them back; and there was a smile on her lips. The Lady Dorothea was not one to burden her lover with a woman's weakness when he must immediately face cannon and musket and sword.

The Count of Organdie returned her smile gaily. One could hardly believe that, only a few moments ago, the colonel of the regiment had strode into the ballroom and said in that gruff, endearing voice of his: "Ladies, forgive me. Gentlemen, the enemy has crossed our frontier. It is our duty to ride and to stand firm at the Crimson River until the Grand Army relieves us. Gentlemen, we are, I believe, one regiment against nine, but we know our duty. The enemy shall not pass by us nor, by the grace of God, shall he pass over us . . . Take your partners for the last waltz."

And there was the Count, so young, so fearless. And there was the Lady Dorothea, bravely concealing the dread in her heart.

And there was the door-buzz, adding neurotic syncopation to the glorious music of Strauss.

Dr. Slink heard it and froze momentarily. Then, with lightning speed, she kissed the Count of Organdie and despatched him to the wars. At the same time, she dealt with matters practical. She cancelled the tape, snatched a green quilted cat-suit, zipped herself in and, as an afterthought, slipped the freezair pencil into a concealed pocket.

Finally, she went to the door and peered through the wide-angle spy lens.

The face on the other side was familiar. She released the electro-lock and opened the door.

"Why, Peter, how sweet of you to come! What a gorgeous surprise. Do, do come in."

She opened the door. This time, it really was Peter. He came in.

"Dear Dorothea. You look more lovely than ever." He sighed. "One of these days I hope to be free to say things to you that ..." There was no need to enlarge further. Dr. Slink was in thrall.

"If I had known you were coming, I would have worn something special. Do sit down." With perfect hostessmanship, she offered him the genuine replica J.F.K. rocking chair. Peter Karamazov sat down.

"Drink?"

"Please."

"On the rocks?"

"On the rocks."

Dr. Slink pressed a stud on her antique book case, and the collected works of Charles Dickens sank to reveal a small array of bottles and glasses. She pressed another stud and Thackeray gave way to the ice compartment. Then she poured two generous measures of Scotch. It would be uncivil not to keep dear Peter company. Besides, the Scotch would help to relax her. The ethereal Count of Organdie was no match for the reality of a handsome secret service agent.

"*Salud.*"

"*À votre santé.*"

"Dorothea?"

"Yes, Peter?" She curled herself up on a real Victorian fauteuil and gazed at him expectantly.

"You recall what we were talking about the other day when we met in the park?"

"I'm so sorry, Peter. I really am. I didn't mean to pour my heart out about my own problems—particularly when you had such a terrible time in Cairo ... I do hope your psychiatrist has cured the amnesia. For one terrible moment, I thought you had completely forgotten me."

Cairo? Psychiatrist? Amnesia? Peter Karamazov was temporarily thrown. The briefing by Ilyich had not included such matters. Perhaps they were irrelevant.

"Er, yes. All is well, thank you. Now, about Professor Greylaw."

"Oh, the poor man! He's dead now. I do hope he didn't kill himself because—"

"Dorothea, I have something to tell you. I was there when he died."

"But—"

"The long arm of coincidence, my dear. The irony of fate that binds the lives of such as you and me together." Suddenly, he realized that he was overdoing it, and came to the point. "I was sent to England to neutralize the activities of a dangerous Russian agent who, I may add, seems to have a confederate working in MicroWar itself."

"My goodness! My goodness!"

"You may well be surprised. My task was rendered even more difficult because we did not know what the agent's assignment was."

"You mean—"

"I mean that a man who operates under the code-name of Dostoievsky was assigned to murder Professor Greylaw ... Had I known this I might have prevented it. Unfortunately, I did not know."

"But this is terrible. Really terrible. I must tell Dr. Perrywit. I must—"

"You must tell no one," he said sternly. "No one is above suspicion. Indeed, I have reason to believe that your Dr. Perrywit is working for the East."

"Impossible." Dr. Slink was trembling. She drank some more whisky, but it didn't seem to have any effect.

"You are the only one I can trust, Dorothea. Much depends upon your discretion and courage. As for your Dr. Perrywit, he is fairly new to MicroWar, isn't he?"

"Yes, Peter."

"What has he been doing recently?"

"He is trying to reduce the overall budget by fifty per cent."

"This means the elimination of certain projects?"

"Yes, Peter."

"And certain people?"

"Yes, Peter."

"Ah!" A triumphant glint came into the eyes of Peter Karamazov. "Doesn't this suggest something, Dorothea? Doesn't it suggest that Dr. Perrywit is, in effect, reducing MicroWar's capabilities?"

Dr. Slink nodded miserably, not trusting herself to speak.

"Also, since Dr. Perrywit was responsible for Professor Greylaw's dismissal, doesn't that suggest that he knew that Project Tranquillity had been successfully completed and that, with the Professor out of the way, it would be easier to ensure that certain interested parties might exclusively enjoy the fruits of his research?"

Again, she did not trust herself to speak.

"Do you know anything about Project Tranquillity, Dorothea?"

"No, Peter. I—I don't think anyone does."

"Except, perhaps, Dr. Perrywit."

"It doesn't seem possible. He seems just as mystified by the project as I am."

"He would, wouldn't he—if he were working for the East?"

"I suppose so."

Peter Karamazov finished his whisky and treated Dr. Slink to a penetrating look. "It is my conviction, Dorothea, that

Professor Greylaw was a great humanitarian. It is my conviction also that he has developed some kind of drug that destroys the desire to kill. After all, you yourself told me how gentle his experimental animals were. I believe you mentioned a rabbit playing with a tiger ... I believe, too, that *They* are prepared to pervert this tremendous discovery. What would happen, for example, if *They* succeeded in spreading this drug in the West—perhaps through reservoirs? We would be at their mercy, would we not?"

"Oh, no! Oh, no!" Dr. Slink had a sudden terrifying vision of Mongol hordes despoiling the very flower of English womanhood. One would prefer death, of course. And yet ... She buried her face in her hands, tormented by unmentionable horrors.

Peter Karamazov rose from the J.F.K. rocking chair and knelt by Dr. Slink's fauteuil. He put his arms round her shoulders. Gently. Chastely. "There, little one. Nothing terrible has happened yet. At least, I think not. But you must help me. It is for the good of our two great countries."

"What do you want me to do?" she whispered.

"My dear, you are now involved in the most delicate and vital assignment I have undertaken. There is danger. I will not disguise the fact. There is danger ... First and most important, say nothing to anyone. We do not yet know how deeply MicroWar has been penetrated. I suspect Dr. Perrywit, but suspicion is not enough. Therefore, you will be my eyes and ears. You will, if possible, search Dr. Perrywit's papers for any reference to Project Tranquillity. You will, when convenient, list his contacts both inside and outside Insect Race. You will do the same for any other colleagues who may be connected with this business. And you will also find out what is to happen to the remaining experimental animals."

"I can tell you about the animals now," said Dr. Slink

eagerly. "I learned only today that Dr. Perrywit plans to give them to the Marquis of Middlehampton."

"So!" Peter Karamazov's eyes glittered. "We have another lead ... Dorothea, I must go now. There is much to do. You are a brave woman, and when the time comes your contribution will be made known."

Dr. Slink stood up: "It is so late," she murmured. "London becomes a jungle at night. There are the students and the bounty hunters and some very nasty groups of children ... You are welcome to stay here, Peter. I—I know you are a gentleman."

Superbly, Peter Karamazov kissed her on the forehead. It was a brotherly kiss; but there was also the merest delightful hint of something more. "Dorothea, I respect you too much to compromise you. Do not be afraid for me. I must do my duty, and I know how to take care of myself."

Dr. Slink went with him to the door. "Take very great care, dear friend."

Again his lips brushed her forehead. Then, with a care-free smile, he was gone.

Dr. Slink reset the electro-lock. She badly needed something to take her mind off those terrible disclosures. She poured herself some more whisky, drank it quickly, then switched on the Strauss waltzes, increased the volume, stepped out of the quilted cat-suit and went to bed.

She recalled the Count of Organdie from the Crimson River with a vital despatch for the Grand Duke, so that he could have a few more precious moments with the Lady Dorothea. But the Count had a flesh wound, and he looked just like Peter Karamazov, and the enemy attack had been a feint, and even now Mongol hordes were rapidly approaching the capital ...

And Dr. Slink slept very badly.

# CHAPTER NINE

Gabriel and Camilla were walking hand in hand through the long summer twilight in Epping Forest. Surprisingly, in the confusion that followed the setting off of the fire alarm, they had managed to escape from St. Paul's Cathedral without encountering either priests or procs. Gabriel did not know whether his frenzied button-jabbing had affected any other auto-confession booths; but from the babel they had left behind them, it seemed possible. He relished the thought.

As soon as they were clear of the cathedral area, Gabriel and Camilla had taken the first vacant auto-cab they found. City auto-cabs could be controlled manually or programmed to drive automatically to a number of well-known landmarks and tourist attractions. Gabriel had programmed for Epping Forest simply because it was well away from the scene of the crime. Also, he was of the opinion that a half-hour stroll through quiet woodland would be conducive to constructive thought and good for the nerves.

Events were to prove him wrong.

"All right," said Camilla, "you may now say it."

"All right, I will," said Gabriel. "I told you so. The God Machines are rigged."

"Not rigged," Camilla objected. "Just difficult ... Did you really mean what you said in the Spanish Inquisition?"

"About what?"

"About loving me."

"I suppose so ... I don't suppose it is exclusive, though. It is merely that I haven't found anyone else to love."

"My situation, too." She giggled. "Besides, we do have a little something in common, don't we?"

They had reached a clearing in the forest. Gabriel became aware of a noisy throbbing in the sky. He looked up. There was a chopper somewhere fairly close, but he could not see it. Probably a proc chopper on routine patrol. These days, the procs kept most lonely places under regular surveillance. They had to. The crime curve had jumped right off the top of the graph.

"Good evening, gentlefolk," said a pleasant, male voice. "How nice to encounter young romantics at such a time in such a solitary glade."

Gabriel and Camilla spun round. Two or three paces behind them was a tall, bearded man of perhaps fifty. He wore an ancient solar helmet, a monocle, a caftan and sandals. He also carried a jump wand, but he was clearly not a proc.

"Good evening," said Gabriel warily, "we were just about to rejoin our friends."

"How sad," murmured the student, "I had hoped that we might converse a little. Also, I do not perceive your friends. However, allow me to remedy the loss by summoning friends of my own." He whistled.

Four other students came into the clearing, one from each

side. They walked slowly and purposefully towards Gabriel and Camilla.

"Are you sure you will not stay and converse?" enquired the bearded individual. "I am sure we will do our best to entertain you—after our fashion."

The proc chopper—if it was a proc chopper—sounded much nearer. Gabriel glanced up, but there was still nothing to be seen. Rot the procs! Never there when you need them. Always there when you don't.

The advancing students were mature men in their thirties and forties, each as incongruously dressed as the one who was evidently their leader. One of them sported a Rommel cap, a pirate patch, and an antique Salvation Army tunic. Another wore a Sikh turban with purple blouse and *Lederhosen*. They were all decidedly picturesque. And sinister.

Gabriel could still hear the chopper. It must either be circling or hovering somewhere. He searched the patch of sky frantically; but there was nothing to be seen, and little hope of help descending from the heavens.

The man in the solar helmet followed Gabriel's gaze. "The good people upstairs seem to be somewhat coy," he observed. "I fear we do not interest them. Never mind. The encounter will be all the more valued for being more intimate."

"I'm afraid we don't have much money," said Gabriel desperately. "Perhaps if we give you what we have ..."

"I am desolated," said the solar helmet, "we are all desolated by your temporary lack of means. On behalf of my comrades, I would like to make you a small gift. How much shall we say—ten pounds, twenty? One hates to think of a bright boyo being short of funds when in the company of such an attractive damosel."

Gabriel could just see the chopper now. It was at an altitude of perhaps five hundred metres, hovering above the tree line not more than about two hundred metres away.

"I don't want any money, thank you." The presence of the helicopter made him feel a little more secure. "I really think we should be going."

"He really thinks they should be going," observed the *Lederhosen*.

"Discourteous," pronounced the Rommel cap.

"Brothers, brothers!" said the solar helmet. "Let us not be uncharitable. Perhaps the young gentleman does not clearly understand the rules of hospitality." He turned to Gabriel. "*We* offered *you* a trifling gift, which it was your pleasure to reject. Surely—nay, reasonably, even—it is fitting that you should offer us something in return."

Gabriel walked into the trap. "But I have nothing you could want."

"He is too modest," said the solar helmet, glancing significantly at Camilla.

"Thoughtless, even," added a hitherto silent man, wearing a Mao tunic.

"Unchivalrous, withal," decided Rommel cap.

Camilla sighed. "It's no use, Gabriel. They are going to have their fun whatever you say or do ... Just don't get yourself hurt, that's all."

"Ah, the practicality of the feminine mind," enthused the *Lederhosen*. He smiled benignly at Gabriel. "You see, brother, there really is something you have that we need. As a Christian gentleman, it behoves you to share your good fortune."

Gabriel prayed for the goddam chopper to move in. It didn't. It hung in the sky as if suspended from a wire.

"Eeeny meeny miny mo, catch a coloured person by his toe," remarked the solar helmet. "I think we may interpret our young friend's silence as shy acceptance of the situation. Now, which of us should enjoy the damosel's tender atten-

73

tions first? As your unworthy leader, I believe I claim precedence. But there is an additional qualification. I was a dropout in experimental biology ... Many moons ago, of course."

There was nothing to do, thought Gabriel dully. But, hell and Shakespeare, one could not just do nothing. He made the mistake of doing something. He flung himself bodily at the bearded man in the solar helmet.

He never reached target. Somebody grabbed an arm. Somebody dived at his legs. He went down with a bump that knocked all the wind out of him. And there he lay, flat on his face, with two students sitting heavily on his back. With an effort he raised his head. He could just see Camilla's legs. And those of the bearded student. Close.

There was no sound for a few dreadful moments. Then there was the sound of tearing. Camilla's shift fell round her ankles. The bra came next. Then she was pushed bodily down to the grass.

The bearded student did not bother to remove her tights. He merely tore them in the appropriate place. Then he took off his solar helmet, hitched up his caftan and proceeded to rape her.

Camilla was frightened, and the grass was uncomfortable, and the student was heavy and energetic and smelt of garlic. But the experience, she was interested to discover, was not altogether terrifying nor unbearably repulsive. She had got off to a cold and slightly painful start. But soon she was amazed to find that her body, at least, was beginning to respond with restrained enthusiasm.

She could not see Gabriel. She could only see close-ups of hairy face and intermittent patches of sky. But she knew Gabriel was being forced to watch. She felt dreadfully sorry for him—in an oddly maternal sort of way.

But her capacity for independent thought began to cloud

74

over as the student got into top gear. He was no great shakes as a lover, but he knew what to do to a woman's body to achieve a modicum of efficient sexuality ... If you can't resist 'em, join 'em and get it over with. Camilla's tongue popped out and her eyes rolled, and she even forgot to wish she wasn't in the prommy phase.

"Struggle a bit," whispered the student into her ear. "Blast your sweet buttocks, struggle a bit."

"I can't," she panted, "you're too damn heavy."

"I'll take some of the weight off," he panted, "but—if—if you don't—put on a decent show—I—I'll—start biting."

But he didn't have time to start biting, because a blank look came over his face and his body tensed and throbbed, tensed and throbbed for obvious biological reasons.

Greatly to her surprise, Camilla arrived at the same time. She thought obscurely that it was just like two strangers bumping into each other in a fog.

The student collected his wits, removed himself and picked up his solar helmet. He didn't seem inclined to say anything more. Perhaps there was nothing more to say.

Camilla did not attempt to get up. Clearly, there was little point in making the effort. But in the few seconds it took for the man with the Rommel cap to loosen his Salvation Army gear, she managed to roll over so that she could see Gabriel and give him an encouraging smile.

"Don't take it to heart, love," she gasped, making the effort to smile. "I was introduced to this sort of thing before I was sixteen."

Gabriel had stopped struggling. It wasn't getting him anywhere. There was an agonized expression on his face that was oddly comical. Camilla thought that he looked as if he had tooth-ache. He was trying to say something; but the students on his back bounced about a little, and the only sound that emerged was a painful wheeze.

"I believe," said rapist number two, removing his Rommel cap with a flourish, "that the next dance is mine."

He looked down at Camilla almost benignly for a moment, then he flung himself upon her. He was, if anything, more energetic than the man with the solar helmet. Camilla was tired and depressed and more unhappy for Gabriel than for herself; but her body did not seem to care about such matters. The million-year programming was more potent than fatigue or unhappiness, more potent even than prejudice or conceptual thought. Its frenzied response took her personality once more into a cloud of unbeing. Her breasts and thighs strained, her eyes widened, becoming briefly vacant, and she was aware that, a long way away, somebody was saying something to her. Something about struggling. But it didn't matter because she was struggling. She was struggling to avoid drowning. And then, again, there was the mindless crisis, the locked jerky movements of automata. And then the tension went, the hardness dissolved, the weight lifted and it was all over.

She didn't want to look at Gabriel this time. She didn't want to do anything but lie there, legs and arms spread out, listening to her heart-beats, feeling the sweat roll down her face, getting her breath.

She didn't even bother to look who the next one was. It didn't seem to matter. All that mattered was that, incredibly, her body seemed willing to participate in the big bad joke all over again.

Democratically, as the students took turn to rape Camilla, they also took turns to sit heavily on Gabriel. He, too, was feeling the strain.

While the last student indulged himself, Camilla blissfully went to sleep or fainted. Or both. He slapped her face briskly until she opened her eyes. Clearly he was not at all enchanted with the notion of going it alone. She knew when he had finished by the fact that a bouncing hundred-kilo weight had been removed from her body, that her legs, breasts, arms, lips could ache without compulsion or interference, that she could try to breathe normally once more and listen with detached interest to the drumming in her head.

There was also a roaring, a strange powerful roaring, and a delicious tornado that seemed to blow life into her. Unhappily, the roaring stopped.

The chopper had landed.

As Camilla realized she was no longer being ravished, Gabriel discovered that he was no longer being sat on. He heard the chopper coming down and tried to stand up; but there was no strength left in his limbs, and he fell down again, cursing and gasping and feeling needles of pain in his muscles.

Presently, he was aware of someone turning him over and helping him to sit up. It was a beautiful girl wearing a short white chemise. She gave him something to drink. He drank greedily. And pain dissolved, and fire and energy surged through his limbs. Camilla also was sitting up, being given something to drink by a girl in a white chemise.

Gabriel smiled gratefully at Camilla. She smiled gratefully back. Each was grateful that the other was alive and reasonably well.

Then Gabriel looked at the chopper which, though it had arrived too late to prevent, had at least arrived not too late to cure.

It wasn't a proc chopper. It wasn't even a medic chopper. It was a NaTel chopper.

The penny dropped.

Gabriel jumped to his feet, his head exploding with notions of mass-murder. Unfortunately, his muscles were not equal to his intentions, and he fell in a heap once more. Unfortunately also, it only took seconds for the massive dose of booster-tranquilizer he had been given to take effect.

77

"Relax, honey," said the NaTel nurse, "everything is going to be fine. You both get lead fees, hazard allowance, physical injury compensation, mental agony percentage and another fifty per cent of lead fee for Eurovision transmission. The same, too, for any Stateside deal. Lover boy, you're both in rich red clover. Altogether, it can't be less than five thousand. And for repeats, you—"

"Stupid, transistorized cow," said Gabriel, gently smiling, struggling hopelessly against the tranquillizer. "Black-hearted female gitt. Goggle bitch. Frugging frigid fish."

The NaTel nurse stroked his forehead gently. "There, darling. It's all over. The shooting's stopped. The little lady lives. And soon it will be raining folding money all over you both. Ride with the tide, sweetie. Ride with the tide."

Almost apologetically, Gabriel pushed the NaTel nurse to one side and crawled on all fours to Camilla. She was naked and just about to struggle into a new set of clothes provided by NaTel. He kissed her gently. He kissed the bruised breasts, the scratched shoulders, the haggard cheeks. Then very carefully he helped her dress.

"You know?" he asked.

She nodded, gazing without expression towards the chopper. The producer or somesuch was paying off the students, the camera laddies were smoking and pinching the bottoms of scurrying NaTel hostesses. A portable table and chairs had been brought out of the chopper, glasses and canapés also had materialized, magnums of champagne were cooling in large vulgar buckets. There was even a butane filled candelabrum.

Suddenly, Camilla began to laugh. She laughed loudly and helplessly.

A big bronzed man in a dinner jacket and with a long thin cigar stuck in his face turned and gazed at her curiously. Then he walked towards her. Gabriel helped Camilla to stand up. She was still laughing and swaying perceptibly.

"Dennis Progg, This Is Your World." His face blossomed behind the cigar into a vast plastic smile. "Baby, you were great. We got thirteen minutes of chair glue. With intros, reactions and post-mortem, we got twenty-five minutes of compulsion at peak spot for fifteen, twenty mill U.K. God knows how many Eurovision, Stateside, etc. You got to make a mark, acknowledge cheque for six thousand five each, sign injury and mental distress waiver, then we all hit champers and cavvy. Howzat?"

"Tell me something," said Gabriel softly, unable even to feel angry that a great volcano of hatred and blood-lust had been plugged by tranquillizer, "why? What the hell is it all about?"

"You were great, too, fella," said Dennis Progg. "Really great. I mean that. You were both just great … Ever take in This Is Your World?"

"Thank God, never."

Dennis Progg sighed. "You're losing something. This Is Your World is a 'gramme designed to make mature, responsible, feeling people alive to the realities of life. It opens dimensions of experience. You are there when it happens. You are involved." He turned to Camilla. "The students weren't just raping you, darling. They're going to rape X million women. Nothing but good can come. The menfolk aren't going to forget it. They'll want to get proc strength boosted so that girlies can go out at night again. They're going to pressure parliament for more effective psych action. They're—"

"We get six thousand five hundred each?" interrupted Camilla.

"Yes."

"How much did the students get?" She glanced towards them. Having received payment, they were now fading back into Epping Forest. The man in the solar helmet turned and waved gaily.

"A hundred each ... Sorry we had to use trash, darling. But authenticity and all that. We had pop-guns on them, and we made it clear—no payment if you were damaged."

Again Camilla began to laugh. She turned to Gabriel. "Darling love, what a scream! What a splendid scream! Remember the last thing the God Machine said? And now this. The decision has beed made for us ..."

Gabriel did indeed remember. He remembered vividly. He looked at Camilla with a solemn expression on his face. "And then there were seven," he said.

And suddenly, he, too, was laughing. He flung his arms round Camilla, holding her close, both of them laughing and crying at the greatest, cleanest, funniest, dirtiest joke in the world.

Dennis Progg stared at them. Trauma, he decided. Relief. Joy at six thousand five. Some people!

He looked at the supper table, an oasis of sanity in the crazy wilderness of Epping. It would be a pity to let the champers get warm.

# CHAPTER TEN

Dr. Peregrine Perrywit was in heaven—or, at least, he was reasonably near, being in the NaTel guest bar, enjoying drinks and civilized conversation with the Marquis of Middlehampton and his younger brother, the Games, Contests and Prize Programmes Controller. The Marquis, gracious in condescension and the knowledge that he was being given three big healthy cats, required Dr. Perrywit simply to call him Burt. The NaTel Controller, no less great-hearted in cameraderie, indicated that friends—the gesture was to Dr. Perrywit as a benediction—took some small pleasure in calling him Dirk.

Burt and Dirk—and Peregrine … Intimate, urbane. Also, it was more than gratifying to be in the high reaches of Lulu Tower on a warm summer evening, sipping hock and soda, and gazing idly at framed segments of the whole of London, spread out beneath one's feet like a toy city ready to be trampled. This, thought Dr. Perrywit, was a moment to savour and remember. This was Contact.

Burt dropped some more ice into his Polish white spirit. Never could get the damn stuff cold enough, he thought sadly. That was the trouble with life—everything got too damn warm. Take this jumped-up prolly: he was getting so warm at the thought of drinking with the Marquis that presently he would melt into a sticky mess. Still, for a panther, a tiger and a lion one had to make sacrifices.

"Curious, what-what?" Burt fixed Dr. Perrywit with a disconcertingly blank stare.

Dr. Perrywit was nonplussed. "Er—yes. Quite so. I mean definitely . . . curious."

"I mean to say," went on Burt, who based his dialogue on old movie interpretations of peers' parlance, "whoever heard of a soft tiger *and* a soft lion *and* a soft panther?"

"My—ah—assistant assures me they are definitely—ah—soft," said Dr. Perrywit cautiously.

"How soft?"

"Extremely docile. One might even say timid."

"I have a thought," said Dirk. "I might borrow them for the new We Bust Your Nerve series. You see, we could have the cats leaping round this naked prepube who has been carved up a bit and smeared with blood, and then—"

"Piss off," said Burt evenly. He fixed Peregrine once more. "I say, you MicroWar types haven't been frigging about with them have you? Couldn't stand that."

"Frigging about?" Dr. Perrywit was at a loss.

"Bugs," explained Burt. "Couldn't stand that. Dumb animals and all that rot. Thought MicroWar was rather strong on bugs. Wouldn't want to think there had been any malarky with my soft cats . . . What do you say, Peregrine, old fella? Has MicroWar been bugging my beasties?"

Heaven had become a degree or two less heavenly; and

Dr. Perrywit was feeling just a shade unhappy. Really, the Marquis—Burt—was being almost cavalier in the way he looked a gift-horse in the epiglottis. Who the devil could possibly tell what that idiot Professor Greylaw had been doing over the years? But anyway, Dr. Slink had given her assurance that the animals were clean, healthy and harmless. And Dr. Slink was a conscientious and loyal subordinate. And it would certainly be suicidal at this stage not to give the Marquis—Burt—every possible assurance.

"The animals were, of course, registered as experimental animals," said Dr. Perrywit smoothly. "But, Burt, I can definitely state that they have never been—ah—interfered with. The project for which they were obtained has been terminated. I can assure you absolutely that MicroWar takes the most stringent precautions and would in no circumstances release—"

"Ahoy there, me hearties!" A vast personage in knickerbockers and Norfolk jacket and with a bright red beard slapped the Games, Contests and Prize Programmes Controller on the shoulder just as he was drinking his tomato juice and aquavit. Dirk spluttered and coughed a little but survived. His feelings of murderous hate became instantly translated into a warm smile upon recognizing his assailant as Uncle Dan of Beauties of Mother Nature. Uncle Dan had got himself back in Top T with the Lesbian Witches of Cornwall.

"Well, hello, Uncle," said Dirk. "Cornwall was great. Really. I mean great. I'm told you got twenty-five mill U.K. and—"

"Thirty-two," said Uncle Dan. "A registered thirty-two. It's good to be loved. Now speak me the buddy-boys."

"This is my brother, the Marquis of Middlehampton."

"Hi, Mark."

"And this is Dr. Perrywit."

"Hi, Perry ... Now, what's this with MicroWar?"

"I beg your pardon," said Dr. Perrywit. Heaven, despite the illustrious addition of Uncle Dan, was becoming confusing.

"MicroWar? MicroWar?" boomed Uncle Dan. "Snotty little output in Insect Race. Ran the show myself when I was still slumming. Jesus God, I was the only exobiologist they had ... You in MicroWar, Perry?"

"Yes, sir."

"Drink up and call me Uncle."

Dr. Perrywit received what felt like a karate execution blow between his shoulder blades. The hock and soda poured back into his glass. Heroically, he reversed the process and gasped for air.

"The good old days," sighed Uncle Dan nostalgically. "We had fun. In my last year we developed the asphyxiator virus, disseminant ataxia, and selective leprosy. I had a good, strong team. Except for Greylaw, of course. You know Greylaw, Perry? A droll fellow, but negative."

"He fell under a train a few days ago."

"Ah, yes. He would. Droll, very droll. But negative. And, of course, accident prone. Once made coffee in the lab with a flask of water containing botulinus toxin. Fortunately, somebody then saw him add oxide of arsenic instead of the powdered milk. Yes, a droll fellow. In the end I had to get him out of the way. So I gave him Project Ninety T."

Dr. Perrywit had a sixth sense. It sensed disaster.

"What," he asked in a very small voice, "was Project Ninety T?"

"Call me Uncle."

"Yes, Uncle."

"Project Ninety T—well, I suppose it's before your time. It was the big non-starter, the footsteps on the face of the water lark, the old tranquillity caper. Some fool prollytician on the G bench once asked us to develop a micro-organism to inhibit the aggressive instinct. It can't be done, you know. Endocrine system won't allow it. Anyway, this prollysquawk dreamed his little dreams of knocking war psychology on the head; and MicroWar got its budget boosted. We took the project seriously at first, of course. Turned a few good men loose on it. But no dividend. Not even with simple animals. As I say, you can't go mucking about with endocrine balance without some eventual kick-back. But the G prolly wasn't satisfied. Said Rome wasn't prefabricated in half an hour. Also threatened to reduce budget if we didn't keep the tread-mill rolling. So in the end we just used the project as a pension scheme to keep batty boyos like Greylaw from doing any real damage ... Fell under a train, you say. Droll ... How did we get started on MicroWar?"

Dr. Perrywit meant to say: "We were just talking about some experimental animals I'm presenting to the Marquis." But then all the implications suddenly hit him and he only managed to gibber vaguely, while sweat formed into tiny cold beads on his forehead. Rot Greylaw, rot Uncle Dan, rot the Marquis, rot NaTel, rot God and rot the entire cosmos! But, most of all, rot Greylaw! Because the stupid, cretinous doddering fool had ruined everything. By succeeding.

Uncle Dan, the Marquis and the Games, Contests and Prize Programmes Controller gazed at Dr. Perrywit with concern. He gibbered some more, trying incoherently to apologize for everything, including his existence, while at the same time willing himself to die instantly and pain-lessly.

"Fella's pissed," said the Marquis, wondering how it was possible on hock and soda.

'Ill perhaps," suggested the Games, Contests and Prize Programmes Controller charitably.

"Most likely a bug," remarked Uncle Dan jovially. "Some-

85

times these MicroWar bodies get careless." He noted the shaking of Dr. Perrywit's limbs and the rolling of his eyes. "Symptoms remind me of accelerating locomotor ataxia. I think we ought—" he stopped, confused. The Marquis and his younger brother were already leaving the guest bar.

"Never mind, laddie," said Uncle Dan, as he, too, retreated. "Just hold the fort while I get a couple of meds to trolley you."

With an effort, Dr. Perrywit approached the outer limits of coherence. "Omigod, omigod, omigod!" he said weakly. He needed the tiny pink pills badly, but they were in his office. He spun round twice and fainted.

When he returned to consciousness, he was in a beautifully cool bed in a beautifully cool room. And a beautifully cool Dr. Slink was sitting by his bedside.

"At last, at last," she said cheerfully. "There is nothing to worry about, Dr. Perrywit, nothing at all. The doctors say you have simply been working too hard." She gave him a warm, encouraging smile; while at the same time wondering if, as Peter had almost suggested, he really was an agent working for Dostoievsky and the Mongol hordes. Perhaps, while he was off guard, it would be a good time to test his reaction to a recent and possibly Significant event.

"Now," she said briskly, "you are not to worry about MicroWar. I can run things for a few days. But perhaps there is just one matter you ought to know about. Professor Greylaw's animals in Sussex—they have simply disappeared. Security thinks it may be a student prank and—"

"Omigod!" shrieked Dr. Perrywit. "Omigod, omigod, omigod!"

Mercifully, he lost consciousness once more.

## CHAPTER ELEVEN

Gabriel and Camilla did not return to 1735, Babscastle Boulevard until shortly before sunrise—drunk, exhausted and modestly rich. They had wined and dined with Dennis Progg and the minions of NaTel. They had watched stars wink into life over Epping Forest and then fade into a pale pre-dawn turquoise. They had laughed and cried at the inane and monstrous joke that Eustace had called P 939.

In the wisdom of the wine, Gabriel knew beyond any shadow of doubt what he and Camilla would have to do. Camilla—bless her—had already made an excellent if involuntary start. But she must not be allowed to bear the brunt of what he had suddenly begun to regard as the great P 939 crusade.

Mercifully, the weakness of the flesh was on the side of the righteous. During the course of events, Gabriel managed to lure successively one NaTel nurse and two hostesses briefly away from the champagne and canapés. The ground was damp, but the nurse did not seem to mind too much. Gabriel, working methodically and quickly, was somewhat discountenanced to find starlight reflected in her vacant eyes. It almost deterred him from orgasm. He took the hostesses, one at a time, into the roomy NaTel chopper. The operations did not take long. He could hardly have been missed from the party.

Dennis Progg talked. He talked the night and the champagne away; and he talked Camilla to sleep. In the end, they had to bring her round with needle-juice; and then, the night's work accomplished to NaTel satisfaction and protocol, the chopper obligingly deposited the two new involuntary stars of This Is Your World in Hampstead.

Camilla did not place her thumb in the id ring until the chopper had lifted away. She was sufficiently alert not to wish to interest the genius of This Is Your World in house-trained lions and tigers. Tomorrow, she thought, yawning, no, later today, she and Gabriel would have to decide what to do about the poor creatures.

She need not have concerned herself with the problem. There was no problem. Not a single pacifist animal remained in the house.

Camilla and Gabriel were instantly sober, though still tired. They searched the house, but there was no sign of animals or of illegal entry or exit. In theory, and unless otherwise programmed, the outside doors would respond only to the thumb-print patterns of Camilla and Eustace. Therefore, how could a person or persons unknown have entered? The windows, possibly. But both Camilla and Gabriel were too weary to face a detailed examination. Further, how had the animals been taken away? Though each could have been led docilely on the end of a pink ribbon, it was not a method that had any great recommendation as a reasonable explanation.

Gabriel tried to think, and couldn't. Camilla tried to think, and couldn't. The events of recent hours, beginning with the nerve-shattering debacle at St. Paul's, seemed suddenly to have transformed their brains into masses of quick-setting glue. Wearily, and hand in hand, they went up to the bedroom. The bed was still rumpled from their previous orgy, which seemed now to have taken place millennia ago when the world was young. Camilla was too tired even to take off her NaTel dress. Gabriel tried to help her and failed miserably.

They fell on to the bed and into each other's arms. But, oddly, sleep was difficult. Gabriel yawned, belched, and broke wind in a dying cadenza.

"What is it, love?" Camilla was semi-consciously solicitous.

"I've been thinking."

"What ... what—hokum—have you been thinking?"

"It couldn't be MicroWar."

"No. It couldn't, could it? What couldn't be MicroWar?"

"The animals," mumbled Gabriel. "It ... it couldn't be MicroWar because somebody would have been staked to snatch us also. Logic."

"Logic," agreed Camilla. She yawned fit to swallow herself. "I love you."

"I love you, too ... We'll have to go away."

"Not—haouh—until we have rested ... Darling, what about NaTel?"

"What about NaTel?"

"They ... God, I ache ... They paid to have me raped. Could there be a link?"

Gabriel thought about it, or thought he thought about it. "They paid to have *somebody* raped," he announced at last. "That's different."

"What's ... different?"

"Not NaTel."

89

Camilla suddenly revived sufficiently to laugh. "What a scream it was at St. Paul's! What a scream, darling. An absolutely marvellous scream!"

"Ultrasonic," agreed Gabriel with an eyes-closed grin. "Also a damned close-run thing. Still, we got the message."

"What message?"

Gabriel took a deep breath and did his poor best to imitate that final, demented, high-speed gabble from the Depthorama screen. "Go forth and multiply! Go forth and multiply! Go forth and multiply!"

Then they both fell asleep—laughing.

## CHAPTER TWELVE

Throughout the night, the brothers Karamazov had been driving at high speed towards Scotland in a large covered road vehicle gaily labelled *Cirque Russe*. Every hundred kilometres they stopped the van and changed places, democratically taking turns at the wheel. There was still a coolness between them; but the success of their smoothly executed animal snatches in Sussex and Hampstead had briefly reduced the quotient of mutual mistrust.

It was Ilyich who had conceived the plan for stealing the animals; but it was Peter who had thought of hiring a small Scottish castle where they could be hidden in splendid seclusion. It was Ilyich who had obtained the van; but it was Peter who had invented the *Cirque Russe*. And it was a combined operation that had yielded the means of entry to the zoo in Sussex and the house in Hampstead; for both of them had raided Dr. Slink's office in Lulu Tower. Peter had discovered a set of keys to the Sussex zoo, and Ilyich had found a copy of Professor Greylaw's thumb print in the personnel files.

In retrospect it all seemed like a subtle harmony of motion, like the old days when, working as one, the brothers Karamazov could whip up an instant brush-fire war in the near east or depose a European premier in twenty-four hours from a cold start. Glancing at Ilyich, Peter was almost tempted, as a renewal of faith, to drop the idea of a second Swiss numbered account. But then he recollected once again that Ilyich had a) denied killing Professor Greylaw and b) denied hearing his last words. Again Peter was saddened. There would have to be a second account. If one could not absolutely trust one's identical twin, who in this world could one possibly trust?

The night's drive was fairly uneventful, except that now and then the *Cirque Russe* had to slow down or take small diversions because of multiple crashes, chiefly in the hover lanes, and the occasional pitched battles between procs, meds and bounty hunters.

Most bounty teams operated from high-speed hover wagons; but a few adventurous spirits took the risk of using unlicensed choppers. The really experienced ones could spot a pile-up, drop down, lift the bodies or parts thereof and pull out in little more than three or four minutes. A healthy body with, say, no major organ damage except a scrambled brain, could be worth four thousand pounds in a bulk sale or five thousand in a carve up.

As he watched with professional interest a team of bounty hunters swarm like uniformed locusts over the wreckage of two overturned ground cars and extract three limp bodies before the wheels had stopped spinning, Ilyich reflected that if the bottom ever fell out of the spy market he and Peter, with their talent for organization, would not be without a means of livelihood. But then a shadow came over his face as he thought of Peter. Could Peter still be trusted? How much reliance could one place on a man who, without any provocation, had suddenly become suspicious of his brother? Ilyich sighed regretfully for the fine thing that was now dead. Peter had changed. He had become withdrawn. Perhaps he was planning some kind of double-cross in Scotland. Well, two could play at that game. But that a Karamazov should have to think in terms of protecting himself against a Karamazov. The world was growing older, values were crumbling, there was little that one could believe in any more ...

Shortly before dawn, the *Cirque Russe* turned off the Great North Transit and eventually rolled to a halt in a deserted Yorkshire lane. It was time for the brothers to get some rest. Also, assuming the theft of the animals to have been discovered and assuming their significance to be known or suspected by someone in MicroWar, it would be wiser to lie low during the daylight hours.

The animals were whining miserably in the large van. When he went to inspect them, Peter discovered that one of the panthers had what looked incredibly like tearstains on its face. Moved with pity, he tried to comfort it; but the beast cringed away, and confidence was only partly restored when Ilyich began to dole out the rations of meat.

The lamb they had picked up at Hampstead had become oddly aggressive and was terrifying a poor Bengal tiger. The rabbit disdained its lettuce, and the squirrel would not look at its nuts. Still, minor problems were to be expected. The animals would doubtless settle down when they got to the castle.

After Peter and Ilyich had seen to their charges, they closed the sliding doors in the great van and returned to the control cab to take their own breakfast.

They ate in silence for a while, then Peter said abruptly: "What is the deal, brother?"

Ilyich regarded him suspiciously. "Did we not agree on the

simultaneous approach, brother?"

"Yes, Ilyich. But we do not know the precise value of the animals. We only know that they are the result of MicroWar's Project Tranquillity ... Unless you are hiding something."

"I am hiding nothing," said Ilyich hotly. "But any fool would realize that we have a highly marketable commodity. If that kind of thing can be done to animals, it can also be done to humans. It is for the scientists to discover the mechanism."

"Russian or American?"

"As we agreed—the simultaneous approach. You will tell Cominunder that Socinunder has Tranquillity. I will tell Socinunder that Cominunder has Tranquillity. And each of us will say that the other agent can be bought. Then we shall see."

"Then we shall see," echoed Peter darkly. "As before, the Swiss account?"

"Certainly, whoever collects will use the Swiss account for a half share."

Peter was silent for a moment or two. Then he said softly: "I think I am no longer happy about the Swiss account, brother."

Ilyich whitened. He went red, he felt sick, he felt cold. It was out in the open now. He felt surreptitiously for his ice-needle gun. Peter had obviously rigged something.

Peter saw Ilyich fumbling, and smiled cynically. He already had a small freezair pencil concealed in his hand. He squirted at Ilyich. Ilyich froze. Peter removed the ice-needle gun from his brother's clenched hand.

"You see, I was right not to trust you, brother. You obviously had something rigged."

If he had been able to speak, Ilyich would have voiced precisely the same sentiments.

# CHAPTER THIRTEEN

Gabriel was the first to return to consciousness. Through the uncurtained windows he saw the sun low in the sky. It was late afternoon. Memories came flooding back into his mind. He looked at Camilla, lying by his side, a pale crumpled doll. He tried to rouse her gently, but failed. In the end he had to shake her.

"Wake up. Wake up, darling! For crysake, wake up!"

She opened her eyes and rolled them vaguely, not focussing. Then she went back to sleep.

He shouted at her and shook her, and eventually it paid off.

"Go away," she murmured. "I want to die in my sleep."

"You can't. There isn't enough time. If we don't want trouble in large helpings, I think we have to get out of here fast."

"I ache," she protested. "My legs ache, my breasts ache, my back aches ... I got raped somewhat. Remember?"

"In case you didn't notice, I started a small rapefest myself. But there isn't time to complain. We have to be elsewhere."

"Why?"

"Because whoever snatched the animals may suddenly get interested in us."

She sat up and thought about it. "I can't go anywhere until I've had a bath," she decided. "I am an old woman of ninety-seven, I have been trampled upon by elephants, and there are certain private injuries about which I do not care to speak."

"Then we'll both take baths," he exploded. "And if the goddam Security wallahs come we'll ask them to wait nicely outside the goddam door."

Camilla burst out laughing. "Be sensible, love. We don't know who took the animals. Or why. If it was a Security jape, I'm sure we would have already been trolleyed ... A bath I must have. A bath *we* must have. And while we are having it let's try to think."

Gabriel accepted defeat. But in order to speed matters up a little he ran to the bathroom and turned on the taps. Then he and Camilla struggled out of their crumpled clothes.

He looked at her, noting the bruises and the scratches. He put his arms round her and kissed her gently. "You were absolutely right about the bath. I'll comfort you properly later. As a penance, I will take the shallow end."

The bath was excruciatingly luxurious. Gabriel had added lacings of foam, and he and Camilla sat gazing solemnly at each other across miniature alpine ranges of bubbles.

"How much money have we got?"

"The NaTel scrip, for a start," said Camilla. "That is thirteen thousand. And there is the five thousand Eustace gave me on signature. I never touched it. So we are really quite rich."

"Good. Enough to enable us to lift off and become two lost people. You will probably have to dye your hair, and I will probably have to grow a beard."

Camilla pouted. "I don't see why. I don't see that we have done anything really wrong—unless you count the St. Paul's fiasco."

"I do count St. Paul's. But what is more important is that we are still in possession of stolen bacteria, the property of MicroWar." He grinned. "And so, probably, after last night's efforts are a lot of other people."

Camilla was trying to sculpt a sexy torso in the bath foam. "I don't see that we can be blamed, really. It's all Eustace's fault. He shouldn't have shot me full of P 939."

"Eustace is dead. We are alive. Therefore we can be blamed—especially since we didn't trot along to MicroWar and tell the whole story."

Camilla was silent for a moment or two. Then she said somewhat irrelevantly: "I'm very much in the prommy phase ... I keep wanting it. You would think I'd have had quite enough for a day or two, but I keep wanting it ... Have you reached the prommy phase yet, Gabriel?"

He considered carefully. "Yes, I must have. I did quite a job on those NaTel bitches, but I still want some more."

"Good!"

"If we go on like this," he said gloomily, "we'll kill ourselves."

"Can you think of a better way ... Mind you, I also feel terribly hungry. Perhaps I'm beginning phase two."

Gabriel sighed. "Let's try to concentrate on immediate problems. Did Eustace ever mention the possibility of an antidote?"

"No. He tried to make it resistant to all known antibodies etcetera. He seemed to think he'd done a good job."

"Shit! We are probably stuck with it for ever, then." Suddenly he brightened. "But so, of course, is everyone else."

Camilla giggled. "Through no fault of our own, we're off to a good start. Eustace claimed that the incidence of infection

97

was almost one hundred per cent ... Surely it can only have a good effect. After all, its purpose is to stop people being nasty and violent to each other."

"For it to have a good effect," Gabriel pointed out, "the spread will have to be rapid and universal."

"Human nature," said Camilla solemnly, "will take care of that. The point is, what about us?"

"We certainly don't stay here. We take whatever things you need, then we close the place up to make it look as if you have gone away for a long holiday—which you will have. We must find ourselves an apartment somewhere—probably in London until we have worked out long-term plans. And then, God for Harry, England and St. George, we just have to do our tiny duty."

Camilla's foam torso collapsed and she splashed about with her hands petulantly. Small blobs of foam floated about the bath, some settling on Gabriel's hair and face.

"I think I know what you mean," said Camilla. "It's going to be hard work—but not uninteresting."

Gabriel shrugged. "We ought not to waste any more time here. It's too dangerous. Let's get moving."

Reluctantly, they both stood up and got out of the bath. Gabriel looked at Camilla, steaming and half covered in blobs of foam, and reached for a towel. Then a look of confusion came over his face, and he stared down at a somewhat sudden erection. He dropped the towel.

"Camilla," he said thickly, "I'm sorry. I really am in the prommy phase! What a nuisance!" He held her close, letting their wet foamy bodies shake and arch with a terrible urgency.

"I thought," panted Camilla, "I thought you said we were not to waste any more time."

He laid her gently down on the bathroom floor. Then he lay on top of her, savouring the first warm, strong, compulsive movements of coupling. It felt like the first time for days and days and days.

"This ... isn't ... wasting time," he managed to say almost reasonably. "It's ... it's ... simply ... keeping in training!"

# CHAPTER FOURTEEN

The *Cirque Russe* was still on the Great North Transit, about one hundred and fifty kilometres south of Edinburgh. It was a fine, clear evening; and there was surprisingly little traffic in either the traction or the hover lanes. But Peter Karamazov, though convinced that the risk of discovery was now low, remained unhappy for two reasons. The first was that he would have to do all the driving himself, and the second was that he was beginning to experience vague stirrings of guilt and remorse.

Occasionally, he gave Ilyich, who was lying on the floor of the control cab, booster shots of freezair. While Peter was experiencing a crisis of conscience, Ilyich remained rigid, conscious and full of hate. Each time he received a shot of freezair he tried not to breathe for several seconds, thus minimizing its effect. It was his ambition to get the muscles of one arm sufficiently de-frozen to hit the vehicle's ultra-drive button.

If he could do it at the right moment, there was a reasonable chance that he could take his treacherous brother with him.

Meanwhile, Peter drove along at a sedate hundred and twenty kilometres an hour, wondering if, by chance, he could possibly have been a trifle unjust; and if so, how a reconciliation could be effected. The trouble was that he had a genuine affection for his brother. The trouble also was that, whatever happened from now on, neither could ever trust the other again. Espionage, thought Peter bitterly, was hell.

He began to talk to Ilyich.

"You see, brother, what a sorry condition we are in. Although I may have misjudged you, it is still your fault. You should have been completely honest with me. You should have told me about Professor Greylaw right at the beginning. Then, perhaps, he would not now be dead. Then I would not have been able to suspect you of killing him or of concealing information ... It is a bad business, Ilyich, a bad business. For years we have been brothers and comrades. For years we have been, together, invincible. That such a relationship should be destroyed by a secret tranquillizer. It is ironic, it is tragic, it is bizarre."

Ilyich, speechless, uncomfortable, his head throbbing because of its proximity to the transmission casing, lay on the floor of the cab and seethed. There was little else he could do. Except keep systematically moving two fingers of his left hand, where the muscles were beginning to slacken. He could not look, but he suspected that the hand itself was also moving. In a few more minutes, with luck, there should be some movement in the arm.

Peter could not see the movement of the hand. In any case, though the traffic was slack, he had to keep his eyes on the Great North Transit. But he judged it was time for another squirt of freezair and administered it expertly without taking his gaze from the road ahead. Ilyich held his breath once more and waited patiently.

"Nevertheless, brother," went on Peter, "there may be a solution to our problem. Suppose I keep you, let us say lightly restrained, in the castle while I conduct negotiations with Cominunder and Socinunder. Let us then suppose that a satisfactory bid is received and the payment made. Let us further suppose that I jet briefly to Switzerland, transfer half of the funds in the numbered account; and finally, as a gesture of good faith I—"

But Ilyich was never to learn what the gesture of good faith might be. Also he was past caring. Also, in his judgement, the muscles in his left arm were sufficiently flexible for the task he required of them.

With a tremendous effort, and helped by a slight unevenness in the surface of the Transit, he had managed to half roll towards the lower control panel. His left hand moved—it seemed agonizingly slow, but in the darkness of the cab Peter, still talking and doubtless trying to devise some further humiliation, did not appear to notice.

Ilyich pressed the ultra-drive button, praying that the vehicle was on a bend or a gradient. His prayer was doubly answered. It was on both.

With a high, muted whine, the ultra-drive turbine cut in; and the great vehicle surged forward, rapidly accelerating past two hundred kilometres an hour. For four vital seconds, Peter did not know what had happened. And by the time he did, it was already too late.

The *Cirque Russe* left the Transit, passed at high speed over the narrow strip of soft, uneven earth, and attempted to plough through the low, thick ferrocrete crash barrier. The vehicle somersaulted twice and came to rest on its side with the sliding doors buckled outwards.

Miraculously, among the cargo, a panther, a tiger and a rabbit survived. After much whimpering, they emerged through the open doors. The panther panicked and streaked off across the Transit. Its freedom was short-lived, and it wrecked one hover sled and two ground cars. The tiger and the rabbit turned in the right direction and scampered away across open country.

Within minutes, a team of bounty hunters in a hover wagon, directed by a chopper-spotter with computer, radar, sonic and infra-red gear, arrived at the crash area.

It being an ill wind that blows the goods to nobody, the bounty hunters extracted three usable bodies and one pre-pube not yet clinically dead from the tangled mass of ground cars and hover sled. And in the cab of the large vehicle that had jumped the Transit, they found what was left of Peter and Ilyich Karamazov, enfolded touchingly in each other's arms.

## CHAPTER FIFTEEN

Gabriel and Camilla did not have to search for an apartment for long. They were lucky enough to find one in an excellent state of repair, furnished and only recently vacated; its previous tenant, a NaTel bit player, having leaped to his death after being written out of the ever-popular Carnation Street, the first NaTel serial to have reached its golden jubilee.

The apartment was on the twenty-fifth storey in Margot Fonteyn House, Shepherd's Bush; and the fact that the previous tenant had taken the quick way down only five days before did not unduly disturb either Camilla or Gabriel. They had weighty problems to consider—problems relating to strategy, obscurity and sheer survival.

Margot Fonteyn House was an unpretentious, respectably anonymous hive in an unpretentious, respectably anonymous district; and presumably occupied by unpretentious, respectably anonymous people. The nameplates on their neighbours' apartments reinforced Gabriel in his conviction that the hive was as good a place as any in which to be discreetly lost. The neighbour on the left was Señor Manuel Labore, *chargé d'affaires* to the Republic of Tierra del Fuego, recently recognized by U.N. The neighbour on the right was simply a Dr. D. Slink.

In the interests of security and convenience Camilla and Gabriel decided to be married on a one-year contract. Camilla had her hair coloured deep red, Gabriel had his pigmentation darkened to Anglo-Indian, then they went to the nearest contract office and emerged ten minutes later with a non-indemnity agreement whose main value was that, in the event of a sad encounter with the law, neither could be compelled to give evidence against the other.

Dr. Slink noted that her new neighbours were a nice young married couple, Gabriel and Camilla Crome. It was so refreshing. Hardly anybody bothered to get married these days unless they wanted to gain control of their children. But Mr. and Mrs. Crome did not seem to have any children and so they must truly love each other. Perhaps they were on a life contract—till death us do spare parts. It would be so romantic. She resolved to ask them to take tea with her as soon as possible. Then she would find out.

Meanwhile, the newlyweds settled in their new home, rested for a day or two—if frequent love-making could be so described—and worked out their strategy. Gabriel made a trip to Soho and contacted an InSex pusher. After some prolonged negotiation in a bar, he managed to buy the pusher's entire current stock, one hundred and fifty tiny, tasteless, soluble tablets, for only one thousand pounds.

It was a great stroke of luck. Neither Gabriel nor Camilla needed InSex; but it was probable that some of their targets would. Camilla, with some relish, preferred to think of the men she intended to infect as victims. Gabriel preferred to class their common prey as targets. It was, he said, more clinical.

One problem in the campaign to spread P 939 would be the time factor. Though some people would always be ready to go to bed with strangers at short notice, there were many quaint enough to need talking down, or a meal or a bath or a theatre or time to get drunk or time to get sober first. With such cases, the InSex tablets would dramatically increase productivity.

Instant Sex, the most potent known aphrodisiac, until recently and for reasons best known to the biochemists could only be derived from the urine of pregnant mares. Further, it took distillation and centrifugal fractimation from the urine of two hundred pregnant mares to provide one good InSex shot. Difficulty was added by the discovery that only mares grazing in the foothills of the Andes yielded InSex that was effective for all people of all ages—not excluding prepubes—in all seasons.

Until recently, the taking or giving of InSex had been a privilege of the wealthy, occasioning much interest, drollery and even satisfaction in fashionable circles. There was the memorable occasion when Cardinal Archbishop Cyril Cantuar had been slipped a shot before the Romaprot annual general meeting in the Vatican, and had attempted to ravish a Dutch cardinal (female) during a show of hands.

But the discovery by the Nobel prizewinner Jawaharlal Schmidt that the InSex steroids could be derived from the Tibetan yak and the Indian ox with or without pregnancy and whether grazing in the Hindu Kush or Regent's Park knocked a zero off the price of InSex and brought it within reach of urbies, prollies, students and all manner of riff-raff.

Which, according to the Lords, Commons, Romaprot executives and practically all the upper income bracket crowd, was bad. As indeed, it might be. So the God Machines uttered, the

Government legislated and InSex became illegal.

The trouble was that the Instant Sex tablet normally produced an intense sexual desire within four minutes of ingestion. Which was fun for the upper classes, but full of grave consequences as far as lesser mortals were concerned. An upper echelon NaTel InSex orgy was, by definition, harmless; but with the reduction in cost any nasty little prolly could surreptitiously lace an upper girl's drink and make her fight to get herself ravished.

Would you want your daughter to want to want it with a student?

No.

Therefore, the charge for illegal possession of InSex by male or female automatically became attempted rape if discovered before and simple rape if discovered after.

Gabriel proudly carried back to Margot Fonteyn House one hundred and fifty potential charges of rape. He was not without apprehension, since a slip-up or a proc raid would probably put him and Camilla into the Bad House for life plus ten. But, for better or worse, Eustace Greylaw had handed on the torch; and somebody had to spread the conflagration.

# CHAPTER SIXTEEN

Dr. Perrywit, having recovered from his contretemps in the presence of Burt, Dirk and Uncle Dan, decided to confess all. He had his standards. He could no longer keep the knowledge of his own carelessness or of Professor Greylaw's success to himself.

That Professor Greylaw had succeeded with the Tranquillity project there could be no doubt. And it was partly the fault of that idiot Slink woman for being an idiot woman that he had not paid more attention to her reports of conditions at Greylaw's establishment in Sussex. One day, he promised himself, he would ravish the big bitch. If it were the last thing he did. He would give her the merest squirt of freezair, lower her weakly resisting body to the floor, tear that damned virginal cat-suit from those proudly voluptuous breasts and ... and ... and ...

With excruciatingly masochistic satisfaction, on his first day back at work, Dr. Perrywit's very first task was to explain the cause of his recent discomfort to Dr. Slink. While reproving her for not *fully* reporting on Professor Greylaw and his activities, nevertheless as her immediate senior in MicroWar, he was prepared to accept responsibility for the present situation. So, with the nation's interests at heart, he told her, and ignoring the trifle of his own probably ruined career, he would now make a *full* report of the situation to the head of the Microbiological Warfare Division and if necessary to the Minister of International Security and Race Harmony. This thing, he concluded, was big. It was more important than the broken career of a potentially distinguished civil servant; more important, even, than his life and happiness.

Dr. Perrywit was almost surprised by his own nobility.

He was definitely surprised by Dr. Slink's reaction.

"Thank heaven," she said with immense relief, "that you are not an agent of the Mongol hordes."

He looked at her blankly. "What the devil has got into you, woman?"

Dr. Slink was covered with confusion. Her conversation with Peter Karamazov had been in the strictest confidence, and he had told her that there was a foreign agent called Dostoievsky with a confederate working in MicroWar, and he had mentioned that Dr. Perrywit was under suspicion, and it had looked as if the suspicion was justified. Oh, dear, it was all very confusing because here was poor Dr. Perrywit practically blaming himself for everything and preparing to make a full report to the head of MicroWar.

But then a terrible thought crossed her mind. Wouldn't a foreign agent, suspecting he was under suspicion, attempt to divert that suspicion in some way? Could this be what Dr. Perrywit was now doing? Peter had warned her that there was danger. He had told her to be on guard. Oh, dear. Oh, dear. Oh, dear.

"I said: what the devil has got into you, woman?"

Dr. Slink shivered. Was there now a certain subtle menace in Dr. Perrywit's voice? Would he attempt to compel her to reveal her secret knowledge? Dr. Perrywit stood between her and the door. Room and door were soundproofed. Who could possibly hear if she screamed?

Her breasts heaved. Her nostrils flared. Her eyes widened. Her face paled.

Dr. Perrywit took a step towards her. "Dammit, Dorothea, have you lost your tongue?"

"Don't touch me," she hissed. "Don't touch me. How can I be sure that you are not in league with Dostoievsky!"

Dr. Perrywit took another step. Dr. Slink retreated, still facing him, her breasts aching with anxiety, her limbs trembling as she tried not to think of unthinkable horrors.

"What is all this drivel about Mongol hordes and Dostoievsky?"

"You deny it?"

"What is there to deny?"

"So you don't deny it!"

Dr. Perrywit began to feel as if all things reasonable were dissolving. Now, on top of the Greylaw fiasco, his assistant's sanity seemed to be imploding.

"God save us all," roared Dr. Perrywit, "you are talking in riddles, you stupid cow! Now try hard for a moment of coherence and tell me about this Mongol Dostoievsky thing. I have enough trouble without my assistant spiralling round the twist."

Dr. Slink's breasts heaved fit to burst through her cat-suit. Never had a man spoken to her like this before. It was—it was almost like being rough-handled physically. Now she was certain. An Englishman—a true Englishman—would not behave thus to a lady.

"Beast," she breathed, "how does it feel to be a traitor to

the Mother Country?"

Dr. Perrywit tried hopelessly to retain some grip upon a tenuous thread of sanity. "I say, Dorothea," he expostulated, "whatever you are talking about—and I haven't the faintest idea—you have said quite enough. Now let us forget all this drivel and concentrate on practical aspects of the Greylaw affair." He held out his hands, beseeching her to reassume the professional persona he had formerly known.

Dr. Slink misinterpreted his gesture. "Don't touch me! Don't touch me! You will obtain nothing by force." She retreated another couple of steps but, unfortunately, her left foot became entangled with the desk computer cable. She fell backwards, her head striking a glancing blow on the desk on the way down.

Dr. Slink, arms and legs spread out, breasts still heaving, lay flat on her back on the deep pile carpet. Her eyes closed, then opened and rolled, then closed and opened and rolled. One arm clutched briefly, limply and protectively at her bosom, then flopped. Her lips moved. She seemed to sigh deeply.

Thunderstruck, Dr. Perrywit looked at her, registering each delicious tremor in each delicious limb of her supine body. This was more than mortal man could bear. This was what he had always dreamed of.

With a wild cry, he flung himself upon her, tearing viciously at the cat-suit, exposing more and more of that superb ivory flesh. Briefly she seemed to return to full consciousness. Briefly and quite ineffectually she attempted to resist. Then, as Dr. Perrywit turned his attention to the flimsy material protecting those gorgeous thighs, she closed her eyes once more. Her mouth opened, and an irresistible tip of pink tongue protruded.

Dr. Perrywit ripped hastily at his own clothing, then he lay between Dr. Slink's legs and thrust and thrust and thrust ...

And nothing ...

The sweat dripped off his forehead.

He kissed her, he fondled her, he gripped her, he pinched her. He thrust and thrust and thrust.

And nothing. Nothing. Nothing.

Impotent!

Presently Dr. Perrywit detached himself sadly from Dr. Slink, who still lay motionless, breathing somewhat heavily. He was shaking and dripping with sweat. He felt terrible. He needed his pills. He sat on his haunches and began to cry.

Dr. Slink withdrew her tongue, opened her eyes, sat up, and screamed. And *screamed*. And SCREAMED.

Zipping himself up, Dr. Perrywit withdrew hastily from the office. After half an hour and two pink pills, he felt sufficiently in control of himself to seek an interview with Sir Joshua Quartz, head of the Microbiological Warfare Division.

After half an hour Dr. Slink also felt sufficiently in control of herself to seek an interview with the head of the Microbiological Warfare Division.

Dr. Perrywit revealed everything he knew, which was not a great deal, about Professor Greylaw and Project Tranquillity.

Dr. Slink charged Dr. Perrywit with multiple rape.

She also named a gentleman called Dostoievsky.

# CHAPTER SEVENTEEN

For a long, long time Peter Karamazov was not sure when he was conscious and when he was dreaming. This time he thought he was conscious. He was unlucky. He was right.

He was swathed in bandages, and sinister fluids from suspended bottles were drip-feeding through thin transparent pipes into various parts of his anatomy. So this was interrogation, he thought dully. So the gentleman's agreement between East and West had come unstuck, and now the rough stuff was starting. He wondered how long he had been undergoing torture. Well, he could surely take a little more. He would show them what the Karamazov breed was like. In the end, they could only kill him. He would give them nothing of value. Unless the price was right.

Then suddenly fantasy faded, and he remembered it all. He felt like hell. He felt all bust up. He felt as if he had been in a high-speed crash on a trunk transit.

With difficulty he focussed on the man in white standing by the side of the bed.

"Hello, buddy boy," said the stranger genially. "Back from fairyland?"

"Who are you?"

"Dr. Moreau. Chassis-builder, artist, plumber, sculptor, tailor and restorer of life to the grateful. You owe me twelve thousand pounds."

"Where am I?"

"Intensive Care. North Yorkshire Reconstruction Company and Body Bank. I said you owe me—that is, the company—twelve thousand pounds."

Peter tried to concentrate. "Twelve thousand pounds?"

"Twelve thousand pounds. Cash, scrip, certified cheque, stones, bullion, evaluated property, approved foreign currencies, etcetera. We are flexible. Payment on delivery. In a few days you will be available for delivery. U.K. free. Foreign countries, normal air rates plus personnel allowance plus ten per cent *service compris*."

Peter tried to sit up. A hidden hand seemed to be slicing his abdomen in two. He relaxed, conditioned himself not to scream, and waited for the internal agony to subside.

Observing the effort, Dr. Moreau smiled and bet himself the client would faint. He lost.

Presently, Peter Karamazov was able to speak once more. "For what do I owe you twelve thousand pounds?"

Dr. Moreau consulted a small card. "For one heart, one eye, one kidney, two metres of lower intestine, four hundred square centimetres of facial and body skin, three fingers, one foot and ankle, three litres of blood, six bone re-sets, various minor accessories, installation, care and servicing."

"But—but this is preposterous!"

Dr. Moreau beamed jovially at him. "Nonsense. Small time. We once rigged a NaTel exec with one heart, both legs, both eyes, both kidneys, entire stomach and—"

A sudden thought had struck Peter. "Ilyich," he interrupted. "My brother. Where is he? What happened to him?"

"The joker who was wrapped around you in the wreckage?"

"Yes, that would be Ilyich."

"He was the donor." Again Dr. Moreau smiled. "You were lucky, friend. Someone in orbit must have a slight affection for you. It is not often we get the perfect match laid on instanter at normal body temperature. You were very lucky. Without Stinkovitch or whatever, you would now be occupying about nine different fridges."

Peter shuddered. What a judgement this was! What a terrible, grotesque, perverted piece of retribution. If he had not mistrusted Ilyich so much none of this need ever have happened. And now, even in death, Ilyich had given all—or at least generously— to save the life of his unworthy brother.

Crazy thoughts began to rattle around inside the aching head of Peter Karamazov. Could it be that, despite Romaprot, God was not yet wholly dead? Could this be His way of bringing the message of love to a professional sinner? Suddenly, Peter was filled with great emotion. Suddenly, he was so overwhelmed by the knowledge of the power of love that he wanted to die. Sadly, he knew that it was his duty to live. So that Ilyich would not have died in vain. So that others would understand . . .

Back to practicalities. With an effort, he disciplined the strange love that surged inside him so that he could deal more efficiently with the ghoulish Dr. Moreau. The time to indulge in universal love was when was one no longer hampered by drip-feeds.

He treated Dr. Moreau to a weak but triumphant smile. "As you say, the parts you transplanted belonged to my twin brother, Ilyich. Therefore I do not have to pay for them. I have only to pay for installation which, since I understand the

115

process is chiefly automated, should not amount to a great deal of money."

Dr. Moreau sighed. He hoped this was not going to be one of the difficult ones.

"I hope you are not going to be difficult," he said.

"Dr. Moreau, I am a reasonable man, but twelve thousand pounds is a great deal of money. Since Ilyich provided the parts, surely you are only entitled to installation costs?"

"Listen, joker. I'll short-circuit the clever stuff. Who owns Stinkovitch's offal—do you?"

"The name is Ilyich," corrected Peter coldly.

"Don't finesse. I asked you: who owns Stinkovitch's offal—do you?"

"No ... But Ilyich does."

"He doesn't exist; and if he doesn't exist how can he own anything? Hell, we checked for tattoo, medallion or certificate. The body didn't have any. So—first come, first served. That was us—and you."

"What is this about tattoos, medallions and certificates?" enquired Peter plaintively. A few moments ago he had felt confident that Dr. Moreau was in a weak position. But the man seemed sure that he was in a strong position. It was all very disturbing.

"The N.D. tattoo. The N.D. medallion. The N.D. certificate," announced Dr. Moreau triumphantly. "With any one, we are not allowed to touch the meat. That's the law. So your little brother was free turkey."

"Please. I do not understand. What does N.D. mean?"

Dr. Moreau sighed once more and gazed upwards. "Why do I always have to lift more than my share of fucking foreign nationals?" he demanded of the ceiling. There was no answer. He turned to Peter Karamazov once more. "Listen, Charlie. N.D. stands for No Donation. What do you do when jokers' clocks stop these days? You don't bury them because that's illegal because land is valuable. So you donate and then cremate. Unless the joker is one of the quaint ones. If he wants immunity, he pays the standard N.D. tax. Then when he dies, let us say in a transit pile-up the procs collect the meat, cool it for the statutory seven days, run the id through MinMort and sit back. If nobody collects, they then pop him in the hot box, since the departed has already paid his own cremation fee ... Does the flash connect?"

"Partly," said Peter with some despondence. "But please amplify about id and MinMort. It is confusing."

"The identity is checked with the Ministry of Mortality computer, which has coded instructions for the disposal of all N.D. meat. No squawk from MinMort and the departed is shot into the nearest hot box. O.K.?"

"O.K. .... No. I meant not O.K. Not about Ilyich's parts."

"Finders keepers. That's the law."

"Nevertheless," said Peter, "I shall not pay for organs taken from my own brother."

Dr. Moreau beamed. "Good. Glad you see it our way."

Peter was suddenly alarmed at what seemed to be a complete change of attitude. "What do you mean?"

"Have to get the refusal legal and in writing, of course," went on Dr. Moreau smoothly. "No worry. We draw it up. You just sign. Finito."

Peter was even more alarmed. "What *do* you mean?"

"Simple. You refuse payment, we reclaim our goods. One heart, one eye, one kidney, etcetera, etcetera. Then you die. Then we got another eye, another kidney, the entire plumbing system, limbs and a complete skin. Total value to North Yorkshire Reconstruction Company and Body Bank about twenty thousand plus, I'd say. Good business."

In his anxiety, Peter tried to sit up once more. And regretted it bitterly. By the time the band saw of pain had stopped slicing him once more, he was covered in sweat. Dr. Moreau observed the sequence with patience and some satisfaction.

"Please," gasped Peter weakly. "I have reconsidered. I will pay the fee. There is a numbered account in Geneva and—"

"Pity," interrupted Dr. Moreau. "Pity. Nothing personal, but we were naturally hoping for insolvency. So now you give us name of bank, number of account, and authority to enquire if said account contains in excess of, say, fifteen thousand. Confirmation comes, delivery date comes, all systems go ... We have had these Swiss accounts before. Troublesome. Cautious. Discreet. They rarely wire the boodle. So we have to take the body to point of payment. That's why fifteen thousand. Material, installation, freight charges, attendance en route and ten per cent *service compris* ... You happy?"

"Yes," murmured Peter, with tears pouring down his face, "I am happy."

"Fine ... Fine. No more problems. Relax. We take care of everything ... See you at the airport." With a cheery wave, Dr. Moreau left the room.

Peter Karamazov lay on his pillow and stared at the ceiling. He thought of Ilyich and his final sacrifice, and knew it could not be tarnished even by the sordid commercialism of Dr. Moreau. He thought it was the most moving situation he had ever known.

"Brother," he murmured, "even in death we are not divided. And was it not ordained? Was it not all ordained so that I should understand the message of Perfect Love?"

Presently, Peter felt better. Presently, he felt almost happy. Presently he slept.

## CHAPTER EIGHTEEN

Gabriel had decided that he must pay a visit to his studio. There were some things he wanted, and some things he had to do. There ought not to be any problem, he told himself, because thus far there was really no reason why he should be officially connected with the P 939 frolic. Camilla would be the only lead MicroWar had—if, indeed, MicroWar had yet woken up to the fact that it had developed and lost the greatest micro-biological weapon of all time.

The studio was on top of one of the oldest towers in Queensway Village. Originally it had been a small penthouse built as an afterthought on top of the ancient apartment block. As it was an afterthought, the only approaches to it were the fire escape and a narrow metal staircase leading from the top storey up through the roof of the block.

As he climbed the staircase, Gabriel tried to work out how long it was since he had last been home. Only a few days, but it felt like weeks. Life with Camilla, he reflected, had a sort of concentrated quality about it. More interesting events had happened in the last few days than in the preceding year.

There was no id ring on the door of the studio, only a simple lock. Gabriel had his key. He didn't need it. The door was open.

He went inside. No one was there.

But there was evidence of recent occupation in addition to the empty vodka bottles, wine bottles, peanut packets and food cans that Gabriel himself had left. Various items of female underwear hung on a string in the small and decrepit bathroom. Cosmetics seemed to be everywhere. A half-eaten chicken, some cooked meats and two or three bottles of German wine were in the fridge.

In the studio the signs of occupation indicated more subtle intrusion of Gabriel's private world. On his favourite figurine —Nude in Ecstasy, sculptured with loving care from a 1979 edition of the Encyclopaedia of Psychopathology—a small red arrow pointed to the crutch; and on the abdomen above the arrow had been written, "Put it there." Across the buttocks of a larger piece, The Lover, was scrawled, "I hate homosexuals." And on the large expanse of Fertility, a heavily pregnant woman created from the collected works of D. H. Lawrence, there was the legend, "Do not kick against the pricks."

Similar aphorisms had been scribbled on the studio walls, presumably with lipstick: "God is hard"; "Spare the rod and spoil the spasm"; "Onwards and upwards"; "Once more into the breach, dear friends, once more"; "Stiffen the sinews, summon up the blood"; "Love is a phallusy".

For a moment or two, Gabriel was utterly baffled. Then, simultaneously, he heard footsteps on the fire escape and realized who had taken over his studio.

The girl who came in was ultra-petite and still as breathtakingly beautiful as Gabriel remembered. He had once lived with her for six exhausting weeks. She was about nineteen years old and probably the smallest and most dedicated and frigid nymphomaniac in greater London. Her real name was Aurora Perkyn, and she was the daughter of the Father-Dean of Winchester. Gabriel had always called her Messalina.

"Hello, Messalina."

She almost dropped the large bag of groceries she was carrying. From the sounds, it chiefly contained bottles.

"Gabriel! Wet my tights, where have you been, boy? I was lonely."

"I got called away urgently."

"And now you are back?"

"No."

"Thank God for that. I—er—made other arrangements." She laughed. "Vast quantities ... It's O.K. to use your place?"

"Suppose it is not?"

Messalina sighed. "That would be difficult. But Gabriel, darling, I still have to use it. I have been thrown out of everywhere. Don't be tiresome."

"I wouldn't dream of being tiresome ... In any case, you have already made yourself quite at home." He glanced at the graffiti and the plethora of cosmetics.

"Then you don't mind?"

"Of course I bloody mind, not that it matters," he snapped irritably. "But do you have to indulge your retarded I.Q. on my book sculpture? There is a lot of work in those pieces."

"Sweet man," said Messalina, rapidly and efficiently removing all her clothes, "you take yourself far too seriously ... Forgive the bluntness, but I hope you are not staying too long. I'm expecting guests, you see. Nice, fat, meaty guests." She lay on the studio bed—still, by the look of it, unmade from a dozen previous rumplings—and began to manicure her nails.

"No, I shan't be long. I only came to pick up a few personal things." He looked at Messalina, marvelling again at her smallness, the proportions of her figure and the grace with which she managed to do everything. But everything.

She was an alley cat, he reflected. No, a carnivore. No, a sad little child dressed up in a child's body. There were pre-pubes with bigger breasts than Messalina; but he doubted if there was a woman within fifty kilometres filled with such consuming and unquenchable fire.

Suddenly, a thought struck him. A delicious thought. A wonderful thought.

"Messalina, these guests. Have you time to open your legs for me?"

She looked at him with interest. "Darling, what a joke. You swore you'd never lay me again, remember?"

"That was because I loved you."

"You don't love me any more?"

"No."

"That's all right then. It was all rather restricting." Messalina leaned over the side of the bed and fumbled underneath it. She found an apple, a large red apple. "God, I love apples. They are so clean and fresh. Besides, I'm famished. I really must eat something some time ... You don't mind, darling, do you?"

Gabriel, already half undressed, stared at her and raised an eyebrow. Then he shrugged. "No, I don't mind. Don't choke, that's all."

She giggled. "Quite. In the circumstances I think the reverse would be appropriate." She lay on her stomach, raised her head slightly and began to munch the apple.

With considerable effort and restraint, Gabriel did his best not to interfere with Messalina's concentration on her apple. But he was mildly gratified that towards the end for a few moments she stopped munching.

Presently, he withdrew, got off the bed and was immediately and immensely sorry for her. He was sorry for all the fulfilment she had never had and all the fulfilment she would never have.

No doubt there would be many more bodies lying on Messalina before the day ended; but nothing would be achieved, nothing at all. Some day somebody would kill her out of sheer pity because she didn't know what it was to be alive.

He was filled with tenderness. Poor child. No alley cat. No carnivore. Just somebody looking for a golden fleece. Only, for Messalina there never had been any golden fleece. The Father-Dean of Winchester and some clown up in orbit had seen to that.

"That was quite pleasant," sighed Messalina. "Quite, quite pleasant." She put the apple core back under the bed.

Gabriel had the good sense not to ask precisely what she was talking about. He searched himself for money, found about fifty pounds and put it in the grocery bag still lying on the floor.

"Messalina," he said, "you have just joined the army. The cause is just, victory is assured, you will make an excellent soldier, and I hope you have an interesting war."

"Balls," said Messalina. "But thanks for the money. What is all this trip crap? Who's fighting for what?"

"You are—for peace. That is what they always say, isn't it?" He laughed. "Don't worry, little one. You are an invincible one-woman assault division. Hasta la pizza." Gabriel blew her a kiss and left the studio.

# CHAPTER NINETEEN

Sir Joshua Quartz, head of the Microbiological Warfare Division, was in the midst of a rather difficult interview with the Right Honourable Theodore Flower, Minister of International Security and Race Harmony. He had just told the Minister all that he knew of the Greylaw-Perrywit-Slink affair; and the Minister, a Jewish Negro of considerable political power who had been swept into Parliament five times by Midland prollies on a huge guilt-complex vote, was not happy.

He looked severely from behind pebble lenses and a two-metre wide desk at this white trash who had brought him the sorry story.

"It looks grave, Quartz."

"Yes, Minister."

"I may even have to lose you."

"Yes, Minister."

"Think of the newsflash: MicroWar scientist rapes assistant

while Reds snatch peace drug ... Quartz, I'm sorry, but it looks grave. MicroWar reflects on the whole of the Insect Race ... Even I might have to resign. Have you thought of that?"

"No, Minister."

"Then think of it now, laddie. I don't like your attitude."

"I'm sorry, Minister."

Suddenly the Minister of International Security and Race Harmony leaned back in his chair and shot a penetrating look at the head of the Microbiological Warfare Division. He said nothing for a full minute. The sweat formed in tiny beads on Sir Joshua's forehead.

"For some time, laddie," rasped the Minister, "I have had the feeling that you have not been keeping me fully informed. I have had the feeling that there might be something personal ... Don't you approve of Jewish Negroes, Quartz?"

"No—I mean yes. I mean, sir, I think Jewish Negroes are— are people, like other people."

"People like other people!" snorted the Minister. "You are out of your tree, laddie. Or blind. Or both ... So you don't think Jewish Negroes are fit to hold positions of responsibility?"

By this time, Sir Joshua was trembling. "No sir. That is, I think Jewish Negroes are immensely capable people."

The Right Honourable Theodore Flower leaned forward dramatically, and banged the desk with his fist. "But not good enough to be Ministers of the Crown, eh? Is that it?" he barked. Then without giving the head of MicroWar any time to reply, he went on: "I've been thinking about you, Quartz. I've been thinking about you for some time. I've felt you resented me. I've felt you didn't want to co-operate fully. I've felt you were keeping things back ... And there's another aspect, Quartz. How do I know you and maybe some others haven't set this whole goddam box of tricks up just to discredit me?" Again he banged the desk. "No matter. I'm big enough to handle it, Quartz. Big enough to handle it. But I'll just remind you of one thing: while I sit here, I'll have no white trash in my ministry stirring up any racism at all! Is that clear?"

The Minister was gratified to see that his speech had had some small effect. Sir Joshua Quartz was now not only sweating profusely and shaking, he was also silently weeping. The Minister allowed him to suffer for a while, then he said almost gently: "So long as you are really sorry, Quartz. That is the main thing, laddie. Repentance ... Don't take it too hard, now. It may not be necessary to lose you after all."

"Thank you, Minister," sniffed Sir Joshua. "Thank you very much, sir ... There—there remains this matter of the tranquillity drug. Please, sir, would you advise me? I—I feel it is now a matter beyond my competence."

"That's better, old son. Sensible to admit when you are out of your depth. We're friends and colleagues, remember that. We confide in each other. We rely on each other. Isn't that so?"

"Yes, Minister."

"And no hard feelings against Jewish Negroes, eh?"

"No, Minister ... I—I think that Jewish Negroes are sometimes gifted with exceptional abilities."

"So are Romaprot whites," observed the Minister generously. "Hell, they are people, too. Why, some of my best friends are—but let's get down to business. What would *you* do, laddie?"

"About what, Minister?"

"About your pet rapist and the tranquillity drug," snapped the Minister, irritably. "That's what we've been talking about, isn't it?"

"Yes, Minister. I'm sorry ... It—it was in my mind to demand Perrywit's resignation and institute a full scale security hunt. Do you approve, sir?"

"No, Quartz, I do not approve. Put Perrywit out to grass, and there will be further leaks. He'll flog the story to NaTel or InterNews or something like that. Also, a full security investigation will trigger every foreign agent in the country. Then we stand to lose not only the drug but half a dozen other projects as well. Also there will be questions in the House, protests about MicroWar research, speeches at U.N. and quite possibly a new freeze between East and West. Quartz, you have a natural flair for disaster."

"I am sorry, Minister." Sir Joshua looked as if he was about to weep again.

"Now ask me what I propose to do," said the Minister.

"Yes, sir. Thank you. What do you propose to do, sir?"

"I propose to fire the woman—Kink, or whatever she is called—for indecent behaviour during office hours, thus smashing the value of whatever revelations she cares to make. My guess is she'll keep very quiet. Then I propose to have that fool rapist certified insane—which he probably is. Thus we avoid any risk of *habeas corpus* and attendant publicity. Finally, I propose that all records of the project be removed from MicroWar files and that Security be told nothing about anything, except to call off the dogs ... Do you approve, Quartz?"

"Yes, of course, Minister." Sir Joshua swallowed. "But why, sir?"

The Right Honourable Theodore Flower smiled benignly. "I'll tell you why, Quartz. Case one, the Americans lifted the animals. Case two, the Russians lifted them. In either case, they will have to finance the research that isolates the tranquilliser. Or maybe they have already done that. It doesn't matter. The point is, there are enough double agents in both organizations to enable us to get the whole thing back at the right time at the right price. That way, no scandal, no protests, no anything ... What do you think of that, Quartz?"

"Sir," said Sir Joshua, "it is masterly."

The Minister shook his head. "No, Quartz, just plain statesmanship ... Now, laddie, before you go, let us get one thing straight. We live in a democracy, and I personally am proud to be an English Jewish Negro. But what I want you to remember is this: Insect Race in particular has to be, as the Italians say, *sans peur et sans reproche*. So if you ever suspect any white staff of racist sentiments, whatever their rank or seniority, I want you to come straight to me. Got that, Quartz?"

"Yes, Minister."

"You are really sure you don't object to Jewish Negroes in positions of authority?"

"Yes, Minister."

"Good. That will be all, Quartz. Have your man Perrywit certified as soon as possible."

# CHAPTER TWENTY

Camilla was now in phase two of the P 939 cycle—though, curiously, the promiscuous phase did not appear to have waned much—and was now eating a great deal. She was also putting on weight, but at the present rate of increase it would be quite a long time before she need have any worries.

On the day when Gabriel struck a blow for tranquillity with Messalina, Camilla decided to kick off with Señor Manuel Labore, *chargé d'affaires* to the Republic of Tierra del Fuego. It occurred to her that infiltration of the Diplomatic Corps could have far-reaching consequences. Besides, as a neighbour he was a very convenient target. So, having fortified herself with an avocado pear, three lamb cutlets and two cream cakes, she put on a flimsy house tunic, a slight misting of *Je Reviens* and, armed with one InSex tablet in case of emergency, went next door—ostensibly to borrow some coffee.

The InSex proved unnecessary. Señor Manuel Labore was a man of some talent where ladies were concerned. From the preliminary gin and tonic to an energetic if brief exercise on black silk sheets and pillows took less than forty-five minutes. At this rate, thought Camilla, when pulse and respiration had returned to normal, allowing for rest and travelling time, she could probably cope with six similar engagements a day.

Manuel was a darkly handsome young man, who puzzled Camilla by doing his Spanish language thing rather badly. When she asked him about it, he disarmingly confessed all. As it turned out, he was British by birth and had only recently become a Tierra del Fuegan, chiefly because as a *chargé d'affaires* he enjoyed a generous expense allowance, and largely as a result of his frequent connections with the daughter of the Argentine Ambassador to the Court of St. James.

Camilla liked him. She even liked his real name, which was Christopher Crumpet.

As she departed, taking the packet of coffee she did not really need, she said: "Thank you for the coffee, Christopher —and, of course, the hospitality. Perhaps there will be an opportunity to continue our conversation some time."

He pulled a face. "Pliz, señorita," he said atrociously. "I am theenking Manuel. I am theenking Spanish weech I may hef to spik if I ever go to Tierra del Fuego—Madre de Dios and heaven forbid!" A thought seemed suddenly to strike him, and he dropped the Spanish thing. "I say, Camilla, is your husband—disgusting word—waiting for you?"

"No. I rather hope he is busy elsewhere."

"Good. You wouldn't like to go to a diplomatic reception, would you? Horribly boring, really. But free drinks, free food and sometimes interesting people. It's at the Russian Embassy. They are celebrating something or other about an old folk singer called Ivan the Terrible."

Camilla smiled. "Do you know, I really would like to go to

a diplomatic reception. I haven't ever been to one—and, as you say, Christopher, there might be some interesting people."

He sighed. "Pliz, mi amanti, I am theenking Manuel Labore. Pliz to put on zee dress pronto, and I weel attend you. Gracias."

"Give me twenty minutes," said Camilla.

Gabriel returned home late in the evening, rather pleased with himself. Camilla was out, presumably working. He felt somewhat tired and thought that he would make a pot of tea and wait for her in bed. Then, perhaps, when she returned they would compare notes in a cosy aura of domesticity. Such, he thought, were the underestimated and quiet joys of marriage.

Gabriel had some reason to be pleased with himself. After his encounter with Messalina, he had gone to an intimate club called The Flipped Lid, much frequented by artists, pseudo-artists, models and pseudo-models. At The Flipped Lid, he had refreshed himself with cold lager and whisky. He had also made successive and satisfactory arrangements—later fulfilled in a private room—with what in his mature judgement seemed to be the two most promiscuous-looking females present. He had even thought of tackling a third, but then decided to save a little something in case Camilla needed consolation.

She returned to the apartment before the tea was too cold to drink. Lying in bed, looking at her as she undressed, Gabriel was aware of a great surge of affection. Not sex, not romantic nonsense, but affection. Friendship also. Perhaps this really was what marriage was about.

Camilla looked tired. She kissed him. "Tea! What a superbly delicious thought. I shall drink the pot dry and then you will have to make some more ... Had a good day, darling?"

"Not bad," he said modestly. "One guaranteed twenty-four

carat nymphomaniac, two gifted amateurs. How about you?"

"Not bad," said Camilla also modestly. Suddenly, she giggled. "The *chargé d'affaires* of Tierra del Fuego."

"Our neighbour?"

"The very one."

Gabriel grinned. "My nymphomaniac alone outranks your *chargé d'affaires*."

"Plus," said Camilla, "the Swedish military attaché, plus the Spanish cultural consellor, plus the Egyptian ambassador, plus a Russian second secretary. Now who outranks whom?"

Gabriel was amazed, mortified and filled with pride. "Terrific!" he said. "Camilla, I love you. Come to bed."

She yawned and tottered a little. "I love you, too, darling—but damned if I can do anything about it just now. The spirit is willing but the Egyptian ambassador was hell."

"Come to bed," went on Gabriel, "and you shall drink oceans of tea and I shall hold you very tenderly."

"I'd like that," murmured Camilla. "I'd really like that."

As they lay there, with Camilla sipping tea and Gabriel's arm protectively round her shoulder, recounting to each other the day's events, Gabriel became convinced that this really was what marriage was all about.

# CHAPTER TWENTY-ONE

Dr. Slink, seething with outraged womanhood, sat at her desk with a freezair pencil ready to hand and the door electrolocked. She had had no contact with Dr. Perrywit since that unfortunate, unendurable, unthinkable encounter on the carpet. She wished to have no further contact with him ever—except, perhaps, to give evidence at the trial. That such a man—no, such a beast—could brutally knock her down and then, while she was unconscious, work his savage will upon her poor defenceless body ...

Dr. Slink shivered, recalling the sudden and cunning trip, the heavy blow upon her head, the torn clothes, the bruised flesh. She shivered and her breasts began to heave as she felt once more the superhuman strength of her pitiless assailant, and the weight of his evil, lusting manhood. Fortunately, oblivion had shielded her from the worst. Heaven alone knew how many times he had possessed her. Perhaps he had even committed other unspeakable indignities ...

Dr. Slink sat at her desk shivering, her breasts heaving and with strange sensations passing through those parts of her which she always preferred to call the modest zones. She sat waiting for Sir Joshua Quartz, who had promised to bring news to her as soon as he had talked with the Minister. She sat waiting for justice, waiting for vengeance. Waiting for those odd ripplings, those curious aches and spasms to leave her modest zones ...

Perhaps, besides possessing her, that beast had done *things* to her. Perhaps she needed to be examined by a doctor. Or even several doctors. Of course, if they were men it could be embarrassing. But then men were always better doctors than women. Everybody knew that. They were so much more objective and skilful. And even if it was necessary for her to completely expose herself and submit to their probings she would nevertheless endure it for the sake of justice, for the sake of the country—and in the hope that the strange irritations in her modest zones could be relieved.

There was a knock at the door. Dr. Slink grabbed the freezair pencil nervously.

"Who is it?"

"Quartz."

"Forgive me, Sir Joshua. Are you alone?"

"Quite alone."

Dr. Slink released the electro-lock, and Sir Joshua came into her office.

"You have seen the Minister, sir?"

"I have." Sir Joshua was abrupt. His voice was harsh. He had still not entirely recovered from his interview with the Right Honourable Theodore Flower.

"You laid all the facts before him, sir?" Dr. Slink was beginning to feel uneasy about Sir Joshua's attitude. Normally he was quite friendly. But, of course, there was an explanation.

He, too, must be suffering from shock. That such bestiality could occur in MicroWar!

"I gave him your account of the—er—incident. And I also gave him the version and the information supplied by—er—Dr. Perrywit."

Sir Joshua seemed to be floundering. Dr. Slink felt sorry for him. Poor Sir Joshua! How embarrassed he must feel. Dr. Slink felt it was her duty to put him at ease.

"You need not spare my feelings, Sir Joshua," she said bravely. "Although I am but a woman, I do possess certain inner resources. Please do not feel embarrassed. I assure you, you may speak quite freely to me about this terrible tragedy."

"Very well, Dr. Slink." Sir Joshua stroked his nose, cleared his throat and stared through the window. "The Minister and I have considered the entire situation very carefully. Dr. Perrywit's account is at variance with yours: yours is at variance with Dr. Perrywit's. Neither satisfactorily explains what happened. Therefore, always bearing in mind the interests of MicroWar, the Minister and I have formed our conclusions on the slender evidence available."

He cleared his throat once more and gave her a piercing stare. Dr. Slink stood quite still, returning his gaze, white-faced, suddenly mesmerized like a rabbit.

"In our mature judgement," went on Sir Joshua, "your provocative behaviour—which, I may say, has been a matter of departmental concern for some time—was largely responsible for the incidents which took place. It is therefore my painful duty, Dr. Slink, to discharge you from service in the Microbiological Warfare Division—effective immediately. I need hardly remind you that the Official Secrets Act covers *all* that has transpired during your employment. Accordingly I have to request you to vacate this office within one hour, and I bid you a very good day."

Sir Joshua, the sweat forming on his forehead, turned to

the door and made his retreat before the woman could break down. He need not have hurried. Dr. Slink continued to stand there, almost catatonic, without any expression on her face, like a mesmerized rabbit.

Dr. Perrywit was in his own office, idly drawing a series of extravagant female torsos that made the page in his notebook seem like a promising design for club bathroom wallpaper. He did not have a freezair pencil handy, nor had he electro-locked the door. Which omissions, as he later had time to reflect, were grievous ones.

He had been greatly tempted to try to make his peace with Dr. Slink; but discretion had triumphed over temptation. The woman was clearly unbalanced; and though Dr. Perrywit was utterly mortified by his treatment of her he believed that the blame did not entirely lie upon him. In the first instance she should never have provoked him with those deliciously palpitating mountains of flesh; in the second instance she should never have been so stupid as to fall flat on her back; and in the third instance she should not have made those nonsensical accusations in the first instance.

Nevertheless, he was relieved that she had accused him of multiple rape. It was, at least, better than being accused of failing to rape. Despite the inevitable high price, one still had one's image and one's self-respect to consider.

But there were more important matters on Dr. Perrywit's mind than the recent fiasco with Dr. Slink. There was the protection of MicroWar's activities in the cause of peace. Dr. Perrywit felt moderately proud that he had had the courage and the integrity to tell Sir Joshua all he knew of the Greylaw matter. Perhaps his honesty—even at the cost of his career—would be taken into account when the Slink thing came to be settled. Perhaps, if in some way he could be instrumental in recovering the stolen evidence of Professor

Greylaw's success on the Tranquillity project, it might even still be possible for him to remain in MicroWar. Downgraded, of course.

Sir Joshua had promised to send for Dr. Perrywit as soon as the head of MicroWar had consulted the Minister. Dr. Perrywit waited anxiously for the summons. Apart from natural anxiety about his own fate, he wanted to give Sir Joshua a significant item of information that had filled the joke spot in a recent newsflash. The significant item was that a tiger had been killed by a spaniel in North Yorkshire. Clearly, it was one of the missing animals, and had somehow escaped from its abductors. Clearly, their temporary hide-out would be nearby. Clearly, if Security set up a massive hunt in North Yorkshire ...

There was a knock at the door, and Sir Joshua Quartz came into the office. He was followed by three men in white—meds, no doubt. Dr. Perrywit was puzzled. Sir Joshua said nothing and remained in the background. The meds approached the desk.

"You Dr. Peregrine Perrywit?" asked one.

"Yes."

"You're quite sure?"

"Certainly, I'm Dr. Peregrine Perrywit." He looked helplessly at the head of MicroWar. "Sir Joshua will confirm that I am me. What does this mean?"

The med did not answer. He produced a large sheet of paper and turned to his colleagues. "We have now examined him. Are we agreed on our conclusions, gentlemen?"

"We are indeed," said the second med.

"Unanimously," said the third.

The first fumbled in his pockets. "Damn! Anybody got a ball-point?"

"Allow me," said Dr. Perrywit, offering his own.

"Thanks, buster."

One after another, the meds signed the paper. Dr. Perrywit looked at Sir Joshua. Sir Joshua stroked his nose and stared through the window.

Then the first med began to read the paper aloud.

"From Charles, Defender of Romaprot, Governor of NaTel and liege sovereign of this realm," said the med, "to Peregrine Perrywit, citizen—Greetings. Whereas it has been brought to our notice that you, Peregrine Perrywit, are a person lately engaged in most secret and confidential work at an establishment sanctioned and authorized by our loyal Government; and whereas it has been further brought to our notice that you have lately conducted yourself in a manner indicating diminished responsibility; and whereas said diminished responsibility constitutes a threat to the King's Peace and the welfare of our peoples; and whereas on this account we have required three qualified medical and psychiatric practitioners to examine your mental condition; and whereas said medical and psychiatric practitioners have appended their signatures to this document certifying that you are unsound of mind; we now therefore direct and command you to go peaceably to a designated House of Restraint, there to remain during our royal pleasure. This command and committal to be effected under the direction of Theodore Flower, Minister of the Crown and our loyal servant, whose signature is appended herewith. God Save The King. Charles Rex."

Dr. Perrywit was momentarily petrified. Then his mouth opened and closed convulsively several times. He gurgled somewhat.

The med folded the paper and put it in his pocket. "That's it, buster. Now you know you've flipped."

"But—but—but..." Dr. Perrywit found his voice. He looked at Sir Joshua. Sir Joshua continued to look out of the window as if he were unaware of Dr. Perrywit's presence.

"No buts, buster," said one of the meds. "The order said

peaceably. Do you come that way or our way?"

"But, Sir Joshua, Sir Joshua, Sir Joshua!" shrieked Dr. Perrywit. "I have something important to tell you. One of my tigers has been killed by a spaniel!"

At that point a med dexterously squirted freezair. Dr. Perrywit froze. For the first time, Sir Joshua looked at him.

"Sad," observed the first med. "Sad how they always go to pieces."

"Sad," agreed Sir Joshua Quartz, inspecting a rigid Dr. Perrywit. "Very sad."

## CHAPTER TWENTY-TWO

Peter Karamazov sat in the departure lounge at Geneva Airport, moodily sipping his sixth large Japanese whisky and contemplating his newly discovered and terrifyingly beautiful gospel of Perfect Universal Love. He had already paid Dr. Moreau and had now cleared the Swiss Account. His baggage lay by the side of the chair on which he sat. It contained four million Swiss francs in high denomination notes and a toothbrush.

Dennis Progg and the A crew of This Is Your World were also in the departure lounge at Geneva Airport. They were at the bar, making a serious attempt to dispose of its entire stock of champagne and Guinness. They had been shooting a mass-suicide at the International Pet Lovers' Convention, where seventeen bereaved pet lovers had made a pre-death sale of their organs in order to finance research into cat and dog geriatrics. The crew was now waiting for the special NaTel jet to lift them back to London.

Peter ordered another whisky and surveyed the airport lounge. He felt very sad. All these people going from nowhere to nowhere, journeying from the dark into the dark. Their eyes looked empty. They did not understand yet that spiritual fulfilment was the greatest and simplest thing in the world. All you had to do was love everybody, be a brother to all men — and, of course, all women. But these people coming and going in the departure lounge, they did not know about this thing. They did not know that love is life and life is love. They did not know that this was all they needed to know.

The trouble was, thought Peter, downing his whisky and absently getting another, that the world was too materialistic. People valued the wrong things — wealth, rank, possessions, power. Just as he had done before Ilyich had died so that his brother's eyes could be opened . . .

Dennis Progg had noted the sombre gentleman, sitting by himself, brooding, drinking whisky with careless professionalism. Dennis Progg, having himself got outside a litre of champagne and Guinness, was aware of the existence of a sixth sense. It had operated before, and raised him to greatness in NaTel. There was the time when King Charles was entertaining Mao Tse Tung the Third, incognito, at Chou 'n' Raymond's Flip 'n' Strip. Dennis Progg had sensed the tension, not knowing that the King was insisting on Chinese food while Chairman Mao was insisting on steak and chips. The hand-vid was ready when breaking point came and the royal incognito poured sweet and sour sauce over his guest. The video rights were bought from NaTel by nineteen countries, and the original tape finally deposited in the British Museum. And there was the time when the Russian women athletes had had their lemon tea spiked with InSex at the Stockholm Olympics. And . . . Dennis Progg looked at Peter Karamazov; and the sixth sense warned him that something was going to happen.

Cam One had a hand-vid by his glass of black velvet on the bar. Good fellow, Cam One. Professional to his pubics. Dennis Progg nudged him. "Stand by, Oberon," he whispered. "I have a notion you will soon be in business."

Peter Karamazov was not aware of possessing any sixth sense, but he was aware of reaching a decision. A decision for love. All these people, all these empty, hurrying people, lost in their private limbos of lust and avarice, needed an example. That was all they needed—an example. Then they would see that Perfect Universal Love was the answer to all the ills of the world.

Peter disposed of his ninth whisky, picked one of his brief bags up, opened it and stood unsteadily on his chair.

"Five seconds to blast-off, and still counting," whispered Dennis Progg. "Oberon, this is your party." Fortunately Oberon was still sober enough to operate the hand-vid.

Peter Karamazov surveyed the multitude to whom he was about to bring enlightenment. One or two glanced at him with distaste. Most were unaware of their high destiny.

"Strangers," said Peter in a surprisingly strong voice, "comrades, friends, brothers, sisters, children. I speak to you from my heart. I mean, my brother's heart. We are all one family. We must love each other or die. We must give to each other as I give all that I possess to you. I want only to love and be loved. That is all I need to live."

By this time every face in the airport lounge was turned towards him, and three porters were zeroing in for a rapid ejection. Then Peter dipped into his brief bag and hurled a handful of thousand-franc bank-notes into the air. The porters stopped in their tracks as it began to rain money.

"Paper!" shouted Peter. "It is only paper. I do not need it. I need paper only for one thing and this is not absorbent. Man does not live by foreign currency alone. I do not need it! If you think it will bring happiness, take it and be welcome.

need only to love and be loved." He flung another handful
of bank notes into the air, and then another.

The airport lounge became a scene of chaos, as chairs and
tables were overturned, as glasses and bottles were smashed, as
people fought and grovelled and crawled for money. Oberon,
weakening, was about to abandon the hand-vid; but Dennis
Trogg was made of sterner stuff. "Keep that camera rolling,
boy," he hissed, "or I'll unzip your scrotum and pickle your
gonads."

People were now gouging and kicking and biting in their
pursuit of manna bearing the device of the Bank of Switzerland. But, miraculously, Peter Karamazov rode above the
storm. Tears were streaming down his cheeks. He was beginning to suspect that his gesture might not have the effect he
had formerly intended. Nevertheless, and despite the prompt
arrival of the airport police, he continued bravely.

"Brothers, sisters," he implored, scattering further handfuls
of largesse, "if this paper means so much to you, take it—
take it all. But brothers, sisters, do not harm each other. For
then you are harming me also. I want only your love in exchange for mine. The paper is a burden I am glad to lose."

Oddly a number of people had stopped scrabbling for
bank-notes. They stood up to listen. The airport police had
ringed the lounge, so that no one could get out.

Peter took his second brief bag and began to empty that.
"I am happy," he sobbed. "I am happy to lose that which
would have imprisoned me. I will be happy if it can make
you happy. Then we shall be all happy. But I shall be desolate
if it makes you sad." He had finished the money and, strangely, no one was collecting it up. They were all staring at
him.

Then he had an inspiration. "I want to give you everything
I possess. Even my clothes." He began to take off his hat and
coat and jacket. He dropped them. No one touched them.

The airport lounge was curiously still. A woman crossed her self twice, hiccupped, and began to cry. A man with a black eye said brokenly: "Monseigneur, you do us too much honour." A little girl dropped her spiked shoe and her handful of bank-notes, picked up Peter's coat and tried to put it back round his shoulders. He patted her head. She kissed his hand.

"But the only important thing I have to give you is a perfect love," went on Peter. "Brothers, sisters, give it to me also and to each other. Thus shall we find perfect harmony and become ourselves perfect."

The airport police, dazed by events, had come to life sufficiently to begin to collect up the money. People with glazed looks in their eyes were surrendering voluntarily all that they had found. Peter Karamazov had distributed four million Swiss francs. Later, it was discovered that the airport police had collected four million three hundred and thirty-two thousand five hundred Swiss francs; thirty-three thousand French francs; twelve thousand D marks; three thousand and thirty kroner; one thousand eight hundred pounds; seven hundred pesetas and eleven roubles.

And that was the first miracle.

Meanwhile, Peter's inspiration drove him on. "Once I had a sweet brother," he shouted, "whom I did not wholly trust and therefore did not truly love. My mistrust killed him; but even in death we were not divided. He gave me one heart, one eye, one kidney, two metres of lower intestine, some skin, three fingers and a foot and ankle. And now we are one. I give you the message of Perfect Universal Love in his name."

There was a great silence. It was the psychological moment. Dennis Progg signalled to Oberon for close-ups. Then he stepped forward.

"Who are you?" he asked.

Peter Karamazov gave a radiant smile. "I am the son of man."

Dennis Progg was nonplussed. "I mean, sir, who are you really—in the real world?"

He was rewarded by a look of saintly patience. "In this world, my son, I am your brother. But once, in a nightmare world, I was Peter Karamazov, a creature without honour, who forged his own Master's Degree in Creative Brainwashing and became one of the top ten secret agents of the American Committee for International Understanding. A man who recently engaged in stealing one of the great military secrets of all time from Britain, and in doing so brought about the death of his own brother. But now, more important, I am *your* brother. Is this other useless information of any value to you, brother?"

"Brother," said Dennis Progg, "it surely is."

Within two hours Peter Karamazov's moving disclosures in the departure lounge at Geneva Airport were seen by seven hundred million people.

Within two hours and ten minutes there were repercussions.

Washington denied that he was a secret agent.

London denied that he had stolen any military secrets.

And the Vatican denied that he was the Son of Man.

## CHAPTER TWENTY-THREE

Since Camilla had already inducted one neighbour into the great P 939 crusade, it seemed only symmetrical to Gabriel that he should induct the other. So, with one InSex tablet in his pocket and with the determination to use it if necessary, he presented himself at Dr. Slink's door and pressed the buzz button.

The moment the door was opened, he knew that the InSex would be indispensable. Dr. Slink, though amply proportioned and decidedly bouncy in her green quilted cat-suit, was crying. She looked as if she had been crying since the beginning of the world. She looked as if she intended to continue crying until the end of the world. Gabriel felt very sorry for her. Nervously fingering the InSex tablet, he wondered if the operation would be likely to accelerate the crying or cheer her up. Perhaps it would be better if he came back some other time. Like next year.

"I'm terribly sorry to intrude," he began. "I think I have arrived at a bad moment. Perhaps I should—"

"Please," said Dr. Slink. "Forgive me. Do come in. I have been hoping to invite you and your dear wife to take tea with me. But—but—" She closed the door behind Gabriel and began crying again.

Gabriel felt distinctly uncomfortable. "Is there anything I can do to help?"

"No," she sniffed. "How very kind, but no." Then she added dramatically: "There is nothing anyone can do to help. I have been sacrificed—my reputation and career have been sacrificed—on the altar of High Policy. But enough of my troubles. Everyone has a cross to bear. What can I do for you?"

"Well, actually, I only came to borrow some coffee."

"Dear man," said Dr. Slink smiling bravely, "you shall of course have your coffee. But first you must distract me from my cares by taking a quick cup with me. Oh, I forgot! How dreadful of me!" Her brave smile crumpled. "I had completely forgotten about your dear wife. Do you think—"

"My wife is not at home," said Gabriel quickly. He grinned. "Probably she is out buying coffee."

Dr. Slink seemed to cheer up a little. She went to her tiny kitchen and returned presently with a silver tray on which were two china cups and saucers, a jug of cream, a bowl of brown sugar, a pot of coffee and a plateful of digestive biscuits. During her absence, Gabriel had been scowling at the Fragonard reproduction over the mantel-piece. Upon her return, his scowl became a look of admiration.

"*Blindman's Buff*," he said. "A lovely composition. Such romanticism." He sighed. "They don't paint like that any more, do they?"

"I'm so glad you like it." Dr. Slink put the tray down, and stood gazing at the tiny toy figures in their lush, impossible landscape. "Do you know," she confessed, "when I stand and gaze at this picture I can sometimes hear the divine music of Strauss, far, far away."

"And yet," said Gabriel, surreptitiously dropping the InSex tablet in the nearest cup, "there is elemental passion under the romanticism ... Allow me to pour the coffee. It is the least I can do."

Before Dr. Slink could protest, he had handed her a steaming cup of black coffee.

"Sugar? Cream?"

"Sugar only," said Dr. Slink. "Really, I should scold you for depriving me of my duties as hostess. But it is so nice to have someone attentive to one's needs."

Miraculously, Dr. Slink's face was now dry. She started to sip her coffee. Gabriel was relieved that he would only have to talk about Fragonard for about three minutes.

"Poor fellow," said Gabriel. "He spent practically the whole of his life painting little worlds of innocence. Then the French Revolution came, and his market fell through the floor. Do you know, he died almost forgotten in Paris?"

Dr. Slink was enchanted. "You are very knowledgeable. How refreshing. People don't seem to care for beautiful things any more."

"His masterpiece was *The Swing*," went on Gabriel, "but of course, *Nymphs at the Bath* has great charm." He gazed at Dr. Slink hopefully. Was there a glazed look in her eyes?

"Do you find the coffee slightly bitter?" she asked unsteadily.

"No. It's excellent, thank you ... Naturally, one can detect the influence of Tiepolo, particularly in his early work."

"Oh, dear," said Dr. Slink, breathing heavily, "oh, dear. It—it is rather warm, isn't it? I... I... I seem to—how strange —I seem to have an odd desire to take off my clothes." She was trembling and her breasts were heaving and her limbs felt as if they were turning to water. Hot water.

Gabriel noted the symptoms with satisfaction. "Please be informal," he said smoothly. "Mind you, Fragonard was greatly underrated. In many respects he was an excellent visual reporter."

With trembling fingers, Dr. Slink unzipped her quilted cat-suit and let it fall about her ankles. She did not seem to care if Fragonard was an excellent visual reporter. She looked at Gabriel as if she had never seen him before.

"You are my Apollo," she breathed. "You are Pan. You are Priapus. You are the living Adonis! Take me, my beautiful one, my cruel one, my lusty one. Take me! Beat me, bruise me, ravish me, destroy me!"

She launched herself at Gabriel like a missile and locked him in a fierce embrace. They fell down. They rolled on the floor. She tore at his clothes and showered him with kisses.

Gabriel was crushed almost breathless. The InSex had exploded in her like dynamite, and the wretched woman was a blur of erotic movements. He had to hit her quite hard, twice, before she would lie still. Then her eyes clouded, her mouth fell open, and a sort of drowned look came over her face. She began to sigh and moan with pleasure.

Gabriel performed heroically. And then again. And then again.

As Dr. Slink lay beneath him, writhing ecstatically, goading herself towards a fifth or sixth orgasm, her face damp with sweat and her body filled with all the pain of desire, she had a brief revelation.

"Oh, dear," she panted. "Oh, dear! Sir Joshua was right after all. I am a woman of lust ... A—creature of terrible desires ... Oh, dear! It's horrible ... Oh, God, it's wonderful!"

Then she groaned from the very depths of her being, and her whole body stiffened. After an agonizingly glorious minute,

149

she sighed deeply and relaxed. She closed her eyes, and a great smile spread over her face. Thus was demolished all the inhibitions of years of ingrowing virginity.

Gabriel slumped helplessly by her side, semi-conscious.

# CHAPTER TWENTY-FOUR

Time passed, and Camilla began to put on weight—at first in the most delicious places. In theory, the promiscuous phase of the P 939 cycle should have waned as the compulsive eating phase became dominant. And the compulsive eating phase should have waned as the third phase, the condition of hypersensitivity and tranquillity, took over. The separate phases had been reasonably well defined in Eustace Greylaw's animals; but evidently they were not so well defined in the case of human beings.

Gabriel had also now reached phase three; but although P 939 had inhibited the aggressive instinct, both he and Camilla continued to be mildly promiscuous and to eat rather more food than they needed.

The third phase, however, brought changes—sometimes subtle, sometimes startling—in their attitudes and relationship. In the matter of love-making, for example, aggression had formerly played an important if not entirely indispensable part. Now, Gabriel could no longer bear to hurt, ill-treat or assert himself with Camilla, even though her female body—with all the secret age-old programming that lay in its erectile tissue—cried out to be submitted to the pleasure of tolerable pain and the delicious indignities of controlled torment.

Love-making could no longer be a violent contest, a primitive act of aggression, a demonic blend of sadism and sweetness. Now it was no more than a gentle stimulation, a careful caressing—almost an act of mutual masturbation.

Gabriel found it mildly frustrating. They both did. At times, he tried to minimize the effects of P 939 by drinking enough whisky or vodka or whatever to make him forget that he was fulfilling dark needs by doing dark things to a real, living person. But then the love-making was not very successful simply because there was not any awareness of love. And, anyway, Camilla had only to squeal a little, or a wince of pain had only to penetrate the alcoholic mists, for Gabriel to break down and cry.

In desperation, he tried to distract himself by dabbling once more in book sculpture. He went round to his studio to collect a few of the materials he had forgotten on the last visit. Messalina was still in residence, but things were different. Vastly different. She, too, had reached phase three.

The studio was clean and tidy. The graffiti had disappeared, and on the wall there was a large picture of somebody called Brother Peter in a monk's habit.

Messalina had changed greatly. She now wore a simple linen shift and looked more like a Hans Anderson waif than a five-star nymphomaniac. She explained to Gabriel that significant things had been happening to her and to the world.

After a vast sexual orgy that had seemed to last for about ten years but could not have really lasted more than two or three weeks, she had become so hungry that she had spent days and days just gorging. She had in fact made herself so ill with over-eating that she simply couldn't bear the thought of making love for a time. And when she could face it once more, all the terrible urgency seemed to have gone. She didn't want the impossible kicks, she only wanted to be nice to people; and that meant trying to give them what they really needed.

Besides, she had discovered that Brother Peter had revealed himself at Geneva airport, and that he had performed miracles in the process. And, no matter what Romaprot said, he really was the Son of Man. Because he only wanted everybody to love everybody. Which was exactly how Messalina felt.

These days, she confessed, she rarely made love more than ten or twelve times a week. And then only for money.

She spent very little of the money on herself, of course. The bulk of it was devoted to good works and creative projects among the prepubes and the prollies.

Gabriel had already heard of Brother Peter, but he knew very little about him. Except that everybody had denied everything, and that consequently a Perfect Universal Love movement was developing rapidly on the continent.

He did not have the heart to explain to Messalina that what had happened to her was more a result of P 939 than of the revelation of Brother Peter. Besides, she probably would not have believed him.

Sadly, Gabriel collected some of his book-sculpting materials and left the studio. But even in attempting to take up book sculpture once more, he was frustrated. Art itself, apparently, was a kind of aggression. And Gabriel was no longer sufficiently aggressive to create imaginative visions and startling forms out of such as the works of Alfred, Lord Tennyson.

Time passed, and the late Eustace Greylaw's home-made spirochetes continued to spread their seeds of non-aggression even more rapidly than Brother Peter's now large band of followers could spread the message of Perfect Universal Love. Perfect Universal Love began in Geneva and spread out. P 939 began in London and spread out. Eventually, the venereal disease and the sublime philosophy commingled, reinforced each other, and in the process disconcerted large numbers of startled people.

The great audience in the Vanessa Redgrave Stadium was briefly silent. Round one of an international heavyweight wrestling contest was about to begin. The contest was between The Terrible Doctor Mayhem, one hundred and thirty kilos, of London, and Krakatoa, one hundred and nineteen kilos, of Indonesia.

The bout was fixed, and Krakatoa was supposed to take his dive in round four. But there were complications. Although he did not know it, Doctor Mayhem was playing host to P 939. And he was just entering the third phase of the cycle.

The bell rang. The two giants advanced on each other, circling. Krakatoa opened proceedings with a fore-arm smash. Doctor Mayhem blinked but did nothing. Krakatoa then tried to arouse interest with a flying head butt. His opponent grunted and sat down. There was a look of infinite patience, tempered with resignation, on his face. Normally, at this stage, he would have been foaming at the mouth.

Next Krakatoa tried an Irish whip, two postings and a drop-kick. Still Doctor Mayhem did not retaliate. His look of patience had given way to an expression of complete bewilderment, as if he simply could not understand why Krakatoa should be so beastly. The spectators began to boo. Debris was thrown into the ring.

Krakatoa tried a bear hug, during which he whispered the following quiet encouragement: "Listen, swine, I wasn't paid to do all the work. If you don't start something, I'll stamp on your face."

Doctor Mayhem was still reluctant to start anything. Krakatoa dropped him with a throat chop and stamped on his face. Doctor Mayhem cried a little and took a count of seven. The bell rang.

During the interval between rounds, a white-haired old lady threw an empty whisky bottle at Doctor Mayhem. She missed, and the referee had to retire for minor surgery.

Round two was similar to round one. Except that Doctor Mayhem accidentally tripped Krakatoa while trying to defend himself. He instantly helped Krakatoa to his feet, apologized and accepted another fore-arm smash. Fights broke out in the audience. Three fat women battered a young man unconscious (he was also in the third phase) for cheering Doctor Mayhem.

In round three Krakatoa tried a hammer lock, two back-breakers, a posting, several whips and a Boston crab. Doctor Mayhem sniffed copiously but took it all. During the round and the following interval nineteen women, seven men and five prepubes had to be carried by meds and procs from the stadium.

In round four, Krakatoa again tried a bear hug and whispered: "Smash me, bastard, or I'll break three fingers." Doctor Mayhem did not smash him. Krakatoa broke three of his fingers. Doctor Mayhem howled.

Finally, in desperation, Krakatoa tried a high speed charge. If that did not inspire his man, nothing would. Fortunately, Doctor Mayhem at least tried to protect himself. He crouched.

Krakatoa went sailing over his back, over the top of the ropes to take a ten foot fall to the ring side. He collected a broken arm, a broken collarbone and severe concussion. Doctor Mayhem was the winner by a knock-out.

He sat in the ring and wept and wept. Eight procs were hospitalized after defending him from his recent admirers.

Humphrey Bogart Jones was a professional sadist. For several years he had made an excellent living out of beating, whipping, drugging, humiliating and ravishing a number of unfortunate women whose social positions prevented them from obtaining such pleasures in the normal domestic environment.

Humphrey Bogart Jones unfortunately had a client who was infected by P 939 and so passed on the bacterial blessing during the consummation of her own special fantasy, which began with her being anointed with oil then wrapped tightly in polythene sheeting and laid on a tiger-skin rug.

When he was hit by the third phase, Humphrey lost all his clients except three, who were themselves latent sadists. But then they, too, contracted the disease. Presently, Humphrey exhausted his savings. Presently, he was suffering from malnutrition. He tried to commit suicide—but failed because the act required some aggression.

One day he was lucky enough to overbalance while sitting on the edge of his balcony and feeling dreadful about all the unchecked violence in the world and also dizzy with hunger. Fortunately, he had occupied a fifteenth floor apartment.


His Excellency, Mikhail V. Strogov, Ambassador Extracrdinary of the Union of Soviet Socialist Republics to the Court of St. James, was recalled to Moscow and then exiled to Siberia, where his brutal treatment by two notorious women guards occasioned further dissemination of P 939.

Comrade Strogov lost his diplomatic status and was recalled to Russia to face charges of temporary insanity, crimes against the Russian people, conspiracy to overthrow the Communist Party of the Soviet Union, and of being an agent of Western Imperialist Policy.

These charges were occasioned by unauthorized activities in London. During his brief but spectacular career as Ambassador Extraordinary, Comrade Strogov had offered His Majesty's Government a one-thousand year non-aggression pact, six rocket-launching submarines (since the United Kingdom nuclear deterrent was sadly below par) and the Red Army Choir. He had also voted for Miss China in the Miss World Contest, led a protest march on the Indian Embassy for the rehabilitation of the sacred cow and had broken down and wept when interviewed by the venerable Lord David Frost on his NaTel Late Grill Show about the expulsion of two guitar-playing drug addicts from the Soviet Academy of Sciences.

Dame Ariadne Cymbeline-Smith, actress of distinction, retreated into incurable schizophrenia when she discovered that she was no longer able to play Lady Macbeth, Joan of Arc, Lucrezia Borgia and Jocasta in the dramas by William Shakespeare, G. B. Shaw, Edmond de Ritz and Euripides respectively. But what chiefly unhinged her, perhaps, was the knowledge that Peter Pan—the title role of which had rocketed her to fame—was nothing more than a drama of violence, racism and infant depravity.

Dame Ariadne retired voluntarily to the Royal Festival Home for Disturbed Professionals and hardly noticed when, after gentle sedation, she yielded P 939 to the occasional male nurse or doctor in their good-hearted attempts to help her re-establish contact with the real world.

For many years, the Right Honourable Theodore Flower, O.B.E., M.P., Minister of International Security and Race Harmony, and the only English Jewish Negro in the Cabinet, had been accustomed to compel his high-born Scottish wife to massage his neck, scratch his back and kiss his feet before going to bed to submit to the mild marital buffetings it was his pleasure to bestow on her.

Unfortunately, the Minister of Insect Race collected his dose from a mere chit of a girl he had met in a strip-it-'n'-slip-it joint in Soho, while entertaining the vice-president of the U.S.A. Eventually, the girl had taken them both to some bizarre little apartment full of odd bits of paper sculpture. But in the end, it had turned out surprisingly jolly, with each of them taking turns to hold down the other.

Eventually, the vice-president continued on his good-will tour of the world, taking his ration of P 939 with him and giving it a splendidly inter-continental spread.

The Minister of Insect Race stayed in London, discovered after a few weeks that he no longer wanted to have anything at all to do with his high-born Scottish wife, became depressed and applied for the Chiltern Hundreds.

On leaving politics, he started a soup kitchen in Regent's Park for homeless prepubes and was most horribly drowned late one night in his own tomato soup by a bunch of ten year olds high on methylated spirits.

Sir James Fytte-Morris, surgeon to the king, could not bring himself to make the incision necessary to deal with the Marquis of Middlehampton's sudden and acute peritonitis. The Marquis died, the king cancelled polo for two days, and Sir James Fytte-Morris, who had blamelessly collected P 939 from the wife to whom he had been faithful for thirty-seven years, died of a heart attack when rebuked by the British Medical Association.

Time passed. And Professor Eustace Greylaw began to make his posthumous mark upon the world.

# CHAPTER TWENTY-FIVE

Uncle Dan was feeling happy. Life had been good to him. Even on this desolate, windswept Yorkshire hillside with NaTel crews scurrying about and poking hand-vids up everybody's bottom, Uncle Dan was happy. Ever since he had left MicroWar and joined Beauties of Mother Nature, he had been happy. Beauties of Mother Nature was the big time, and ecstasy was a Top T rating. The Lesbian Witches of Cornwall had restored ecstasy; and now it looked as if the Mad Rabbits of Yorkshire would extend it.

The mad rabbits of Yorkshire were an enigma. Nobody knew where they had come from or what had caused them. There were the usual mutation theories, and it had even been claimed that MicroWar had developed a breed of killer rabbits (for possible sabotage of collective farming in Commieland) and that one had somehow escaped. But, even without checking, Uncle Dan knew that MicroWar were not that good.

Strange. Perhaps the little beasties had been dining on carrots drenched with a pesticide which induced unnatural aggression.

Whatever the explanation, the fact remained that the mad rabbits were quite a sensation. They had already killed several sheep, dogs and foxes. And it had been reported only yesterday that they had forced one local farmer to climb up a tree to escape their attentions.

So far NaTel Research had not come up with any reasonable explanation. Three or four months ago, a nature boy — one of Uncle Dan's millions of admirers — had written to the programme about a rabbit attacking and destroying a viper. And since then the number of odd happenings had multiplied. Perhaps the mad rabbits had also multiplied. Perhaps there had been only one killer rabbit — some kind of freak — to begin with.

Research, though being unable to shed light on the origins of mad rabbits, had discovered a further unusual happening, also in Yorkshire. Apparently, some time before the first mad rabbit was sighted, a tiger had been killed by a spaniel not very far away. Uncle Dan had been mildly tempted to work the tiger story into his programme, perhaps hinting at some kind of unnatural upheaval in the animal kingdom, but then he decided against it. Bad vid. You couldn't show a non-existent tiger.

But you could show mad rabbits. Uncle Dan was happy.

There they were, the dear little things, at least a hundred of them, gambolling on the hillside about two hundred metres away. Presently, the NaTel beaters would drive them towards Uncle Dan and the vid crews. Uncle Dan hoped the rabbits would be co-operative. NaTel had supplied a number of small dogs — guaranteed rabbit chasers all — in the hopes that the rabbits would be persuaded to destroy them.

The plan was to drive the rabbits, turn the dogs loose

among them, and get as much of the result on tape as possible. Uncle Dan would speak a small piece with the rabbits approaching in the background. Then, depending how it all went, he could be cut in again at various points.

The day was cold, but Uncle Dan's electrically heated Norfolk jacket kept him wonderfully warm, as also did the three or four triple whiskies he had taken the precaution of consuming. He stroked his bright red beard lovingly. Yes, he reflected, he really was happy. Since leaving MicroWar he had acquired wealth, reputation and twenty million half-witted fans. Life had been good to him. Almost too good.

As he thought briefly of MicroWar, a name floated up from the deeps of memory. Greylaw. Uncle Dan scratched his head. He was puzzled. Why should he think of Greylaw?

Ah, yes, it all came back now. A month or two ago, or was it a year or two—not that it mattered—he had met this MicroWar type in the NaTel bar. Chatted about old times. Greylaw and that damn silly Tranquillity project. Then the MicroWar type fell flat on his face. Probably pissed as a newt.

Uncle Dan's reflections were brought to an end by a signal that the beaters—armed with rattles, cymbals and electronic flash—were driving the rabbits.

Uncle Dan observed proceedings for a moment or two. More than a hundred, he thought. Possibly two hundred. Perhaps the little bastards were popping up out of the ground. The rabbits were moving slowly. They did not seem too concerned about all the noise and the lines of men. But they were beginning to move more quickly now, and were frisking about a bit.

Uncle Dan became anxious. They looked just like ordinary rabbits. In a short time the dogs would be released. What if they just mangled the rabbits? Shit! What a waste of time.

Feeling suddenly depressed, Uncle Dan signalled vid one and got thumbs up. He turned to it with a broad smile on his homely weatherbeaten face.

"Ahoy, there, me hearties!" he boomed genially. "This is your very own Uncle Dan, alone in the desolate wilds of Yorkshire, the real Laurence Olivier country, where Emily Brontë once wrote *The Bride of Frankenstein* and John Braine penned his immortal *Room At the Wuthering Heights*. Yes, folks, we are in country rich with passion and mystery, a surprising land where the rabbits have all gone mad. Join your very own Uncle Dan, and watch yet another beauty of Mother Nature."

The rabbits were now less than fifty metres away. It was time for the dogs. Uncle Dan raised his hand to his beard. Vid one cut to the rabbits. The dogs were let loose.

So was all hell.

The dogs ran at the rabbits. The rabbits surrounded the dogs. The dogs barked and snapped and were permitted a few moments of glorious disbelief before scores of rabbits coolly and systematically leaped at them and, regardless of casualties, kicked and stamped them into the ground. It was all over in a few seconds—with the death howls of the dogs fading into the wind—but it was wonderful vid.

Uncle Dan was happy once more. Life had been good to him.

But Life, alas, as far as Uncle Dan was concerned, had just run out of unnatural generosity. And what followed was also wonderful vid. But not for Beauties of Mother Nature. Only for the Late Late Horrorshow.

Perhaps the death of a few dogs had simply acted as a stimulus to the rabbits' blood lust. Perhaps the mad rabbits did not approve of the cut of Uncle Dan's Norfolk jacket. Perhaps they were offended by his bright red beard. Or perhaps he was simply the next nearest target.

Before anyone could do anything, they charged. Vid one, about five paces from Uncle Dan, had the presence of mind to drop everything and run. Uncle Dan's reactions were slower.

Although he had the advantage of the late dogs in that he already knew that the rabbits were unhinged, like the dogs he simply could not emotionally accept the fact of their unhingement.

He stood and stared.

But not for long. The rabbits were all about him. They made high, curious, squeaky noises like wet fingers rubbed hard on glass. They leaped at his legs, they ran between his feet, and they deliberately tripped him up. He fell heavily, flattening three or four in the process.

But the rest of the rabbits did not seem to care. It was all part of the show. The swarmed all over him, so that he looked like a seething, writhing, screaming mountain of palpitating fur. They kicked him and scratched him and bit him and stamped upon him.

And within less than a minute, while a few brave NaTel souls were clubbing peripheral attackers with vids, tripods and any items of equipment that were handy, the mad rabbits of Yorkshire had kicked a still incredulous Uncle Dan to death.

# CHAPTER TWENTY-SIX

Time passed, and the parasitic spirochete P 939 travelled far, creating its own subtly hidden bacterial empire, moving in mysterious ways its wonders to perform. Time passed, and Brother Peter's message of Perfect Universal Love also continued to expand and, like its tiny bacterial ally, was no respecter of race, colour, creed or religion. Millions of people throughout the world became promiscuous, then gluttonous, then tranquil and then loving. The suicide rate among statesmen, politicians, generals, dictators, revolutionaries and all manner of con men rose alarmingly. Economists, financiers, churchmen and historians (at least, those who remained celibate recluses—and there were still some) gloomily predicted the end of civilization.

At the General Assembly of the United Nations, the representative of the People's Republic of China made a major speech. Before the world, and on behalf of his great country, he pleaded guilty to aggravating the global population explosion, fomenting revolution in capitalist countries, stealing territory from the Union of Soviet Socialist Republics, supplying western countries with fifty billion cans of chow mein, thirty billion cans of fried rice and a million tons of vacuum-packed sweet and sour pork all unfit for human consumption. And on behalf of the Chinese Communist party, he also pleaded guilty to starving the prolific peoples of seven rebellious Chinese provinces, to over-indulgence in the cult of personality in the case of the Mao Tse Tungs One, Two and Three, and to the persistent spreading of empty slogans thinly disguised as distillations of political philosophy.

In reparation, his country offered to sterilize one hundred million Chinese peasants, buy no more cigars from Cuba, allow fifty million qualified Chinese cooks to emigrate to the West, give Mongolia to Russia and Tibet to Tibet, and order twelve million five hundred thousand of the most dedicated members of the Chinese Communist Party to eat their first edition *Thoughts of Chairman Mao*.

American retaliation was swift and efficient. The President of the United States ordered a vast and hastily assembled task force to steam at top speed for China. It consisted of ten aircraft carriers, twenty nuclear-powered submarines, and thirty supertankers. Even before the task force arrived, one thousand American bombers completed five successful missions over the mainland of China with only one casualty— a plane brought down in the sea shortly after take-off by an unusually belligerent albatross.

The bombers made their first run over Peking. They dropped five thousand tons of oral contraceptives, five million fresh frozen ready-to-cook chickens, ten million packets of chewing gum, two thousand tons of sugar, one thousand tons of freeze-dried coffee, one hundred tons of cream, fifty tons of cosmetics, and five tons of marijuana.

Later the task force delivered a further twenty thousand tons of contraceptives, two million tons of canned food, five thousand tractors and ploughs, ten million tons of solid and liquid fertilizers, one hundred million frozen turkeys, two thousand million hamburgers, ten completely portable maternity hospitals and two hundred volunteer Chinese-speaking American psychiatrists.

The Chairman of the Chinese Communist Party resigned and offered to help rebuild a Tibetan monastery. The President of the United States was made an honorary Qualified Chinese Cook (Second Class) and had his face on the cover of *Time* for the third time in three months.

In Berlin one hundred crack East German athletes challenged one hundred crack West German athletes to a wall-smashing contest — hands and sledge-hammers only. The centre of the Wall was carefully determined. The East Germans then started at one end, the West Germans at the other. The East Germans won by low cunning, the liberal consumption of East German vodka and by six metres thirty centimetres of Wall.

The West Germans acknowledged defeat gracefully, and then drank the victors under the table. West Berlin overflowed into East Berlin. East Berlin overflowed into West Berlin. The Volkspolizei resigned to a man. The chairman of the council of state of the German Democratic Republic defected to the West and fulfilled a lifelong ambition by becoming a pastrycook in Munich. The seventy-five year old chancellor of the Federal Republic of Germany died of a heart attack through over-exertion in his promiscuous phase.

The President of the Republic of Israel invited all heads of Arab states to hold their Pan-Arab Conference and fundraising activities for a third Jehad in Tel Aviv. The President of Egypt declined, the President of Syria accepted, the President of Algeria declined, the President of Libya accepted and there were several don't-knows, among them the King of Jordan. As an unfortunate result of this well-intentioned act on the part of Israel, four Arab states declared war on each other. Although fighting remained negligible, feelings rose quite high.

For the first complete year in the history of sport, no referees were injured by flying objects, shot or lynched on any South American football field.

For the first complete year in the history of sport, more than fifty per cent of all international games, contests and tournaments ended in agreed draws.

In Switzerland, Brother Peter was offered the Presidency, and declined. In France, Brother Peter was offered the Presidency, and declined. In Italy, Brother Peter was offered the Presidency, and declined. In Spain he was given a suspended jail sentence for indecent exposure in that he did wear nothing but a loincloth on the Costa del Sol. In the U.S.A. he consented to become the first honorary half-Russian Governor of California in memory of his dear departed brother.

By this time, the Perfect Universal Love movement, existing on entirely unsolicited funds, had become big business, challenging even the might of Romaprot. Throughout Christendom, computerless P.U.L. tabernacles (lacking even such elementary facilities as central-heating, rest-rooms, pools, baths and restaurants) were doing almost as much trade as the big Romaprot churches and cathedrals.

Brother Peter became surrounded by campaign-managers, accountants, public relations officers and even a few disciples.

After a successful tour of Europe, during which he toppled two governments he did not desire to topple and received many millions of francs, D Marks and lire he did not want, his campaign managers decided he would launch a P.U.L. campaign in England, where he did not particularly wish to go.

All he wanted to do now was to go somewhere quiet—like a wilderness, if indeed any were left—be alone and meditate. But, as his accountants assured him with great conviction, Perfect Universal Love had certain moral obligations.

# CHAPTER TWENTY-SEVEN

Camilla and Gabriel were neither happy nor unhappy. They were tranquil. They did not indulge any more in gargantuan feasts, in prolonged orgies of sex or in disseminating P 939 throughout the nation. They were quiescent. Sometimes, in an occasional black mood, Gabriel doubted gloomily if they were still alive.

They slept, they woke, they ate, they exercised, they made love, they went to restaurants or theatres, they came home, they drank tea or hot chocolate and then they slept once more. It was, at least, a cycle of existence. But, Gabriel realized, even cabbages had cycles of existence. He thought that he and Camilla had become cabbages. Cabbages that could talk, demonstrate affection, even make love after a fashion. But still cabbages. He was too tranquil to weep about it.

At the beginning of the P 939 crusade, Gabriel had acquired one hundred and fifty tablets of InSex in the belief that they would be necessary to spread the spirochete of non-aggression with all possible speed. He had greatly over-estimated the sales resistance, prejudice and moral fibre of the public. Once off the ground, as it were, P 939 joyously spread its own metaphorical wings and flapped merrily forth in all directions. Now, as was evident from strange happenings in all parts of the world, Eustace Greylaw's synthetic venereal disease was well on the way to establishing planet-wide control of its host.

Gabriel still illegally possessed well over a hundred tablets of InSex. Occasionally, out of sheer boredom, he and Camilla would use a couple to jazz up their otherwise routine, mechanical and entirely unexciting sex-life. The InSex was potent enough to temporarily override the inhibiting and tranquillizing effect of P 939, so that under its stimulus Gabriel and Camilla would rush at each other like two deprived animals in season, scratching and biting and squeezing each other towards orgasm until the aphrodisiac had run its course. But the sexual mania was brief; and afterwards they were always bitterly sorry, even ashamed, as they tenderly nursed each other's love wounds, recalling with horror the violence that had occasioned them. After such lapses, they would drink hot chocolate and take sleeping pills and go to sleep with their backs towards each other, determined never to indulge in such beastliness again.

But, while supplies of InSex remained, there was always the next time. It was the drug of desperation, their only release from everlasting peace and domestic harmony. Gabriel did not have the heart to flush the tablets away—partly because the original one hundred and fifty had cost one thousand pounds and partly because the occasional bouts of sexual violence they induced were at least breaks in the monotonous round of non-aggression. The only trouble was the unhappiness that came afterwards.

Eventually, Gabriel had an idea. He would sell the remaining tablets back to the pusher in Soho, no doubt at a greatly reduced price. In that way temptation would be removed, and he and Camilla could use the money thus realized to buy expensive and totally unnecessary presents for each other or at least to enjoy a few really sumptuous meals.

Camilla approved of the scheme. But she did not care to allow Gabriel to brave the hazards of Soho alone. It still was, she understood, an area of vice and temptation wherein an unaccompanied and tranquillized ex-book sculptor might find himself exposed to corrupting influences.

So, one warm spring evening, Gabriel and Camilla descended from their twenty-fifth storey apartment in Margot Fonteyn House, Shepherd's Bush, found an auto-cab and programmed it to take them to the West End. Nervously, Gabriel carried the InSex tables in an antique snuff box in his pocket. He hoped it wasn't going to be difficult to find the pusher and fix the price. The charge for illegal possession of InSex was attempted rape.

As the auto-cab sped along the Bayswater Road, Camilla looked out through the window at the dusky twilight settling gently over Kensington Gardens. Hardly anyone was about, and the expanse of grass and trees seemed quite enchanting in the fading light. She had a sudden uncontrollable desire to walk barefoot on the grass. It was a long time since she had walked barefoot on grass. Half a lifetime ago, it seemed.

"Stop the cab, Gabriel."

"Why?"

"It's spring. I want to walk in the park. I want to listen to the birds. I want to feel the grass under my feet. I want to look at the statue of Peter Pan. I want to stroll by the Serpentine."

"What about the InSex? We are supposed to be dumping it for folding money, remember?"

"The InSex can wait. We can always drop it in the water."
She giggled. "It might have an odd effect on the fish ...
Anyway, we don't need the money, really. It was a crazy
idea to try to sell it back ... Yes, that's what we'll do—we'll
drop it in the Serpentine. Then we'll forget all about InSex,
P 939 and everything. Spring is spring is spring."

With a sigh, Gabriel stopped the cab and paid it off. They
got out.

It was, he had to admit, a very fine spring evening—warm
with a delicious after-scent of rain in the air. Odd that he
had not noticed himself that the only possible thing to do
on such an evening was to stroll in the park. He was grateful
to Camilla for reminding him. It was a long time since he
had strolled with her in the park. That, too, was what marriage
was all about.

They walked past Kensington Round Pond, and the twilight deepened. It was indeed a long time since Gabriel had
strolled in the park, because he was pleasantly surprised by
the lack of people.

It was not until they had reached the statue of Peter Pan
that he remembered why lovers did not linger in the tree-
enchanted, grass-held twilight. And by then it was too late.

The prepubes must have been stalking them for several
minutes. Gabriel had been aware of odd little noises, but
had idiotically dismissed them merely as twilight sounds.
When the rush came, he and Camilla were taken completely
by surprise.

The prepubes closed in on them like a human noose,
tightening round them then dragging them to the ground.
Gabriel could not see Camilla, though he could hear her
muffled cries. Prepubes of both sexes were sitting on his legs,
his arms, his chest, his head. Busy little fingers were going
through his pockets.

"No jackpot," piped a thin and possibly female voice. "Only

about thirty in paper money, a clip of cab tokens, and a little box with pills in it. The box might bring a piece of the old folding."

"What are the pissing pills?"

"Dunno."

"Hi, buster." A prepube removed her bottom from Gabriel's face. "What are the pissing pills?"

Gabriel raised his head with an effort. He could see parts of Camilla. She, too, was held down expertly by several prepubes. A very small child sat carelessly on her head. A boy of perhaps twelve was tearing at her dress and pinching her breasts.

"Hi, buster!" The foot connected heavily and painfully with Gabriel's ribs. "About the pissing pills."

"Aspirin," he said cautiously. He was rewarded with another kick.

"That so? Then suck some and get cool."

Gabriel struggled, but cruel little fingers pinched his nostrils, forced his mouth open and popped some InSex tablets in. He did not know how many. He stopped struggling. He began to breathe very heavily. He shivered. He wanted to loosen his clothes. He wanted to die. He felt drunk. His head rattled with terrifyingly erotic images. He felt explosive with desire. He knew he was developing the greatest, the most insatiable, the most implacable erection in the world. He was lost in a red, red mist.

"Holy Beatles!" exclaimed a joyous and childish voice from far, far away. "It's InSex. Give me one!"

"And me!"

"I want it too!"

"Don't drop the pissing box or we lose the pissing InSex!"

"Give a shot each to the titters!"

"Let's feed this joker's dolly."

Briefly the mist cleared for Gabriel. Something demonstrably and violently female lay beneath him. It moved, it writhed, it moaned. It blew desire to a white heat. Gabriel strained and jerked and groaned. The body beneath him was pulled away. Then it writhed and clawed its way back. Or was it another body? He did not know. He did not care. He was surrounded by writhing, gasping, straining bodies. And he did not know and he did not care. The terrible compulsion was all that mattered—all that was real at the centre of a hot dark moist erectile universe.

Mercifully, the overload of InSex did not allow him to remain even semi-conscious for long. He slipped down into a pulsing limbo, his body jerking mechanically long after his mind had surrendered to oblivion.

When at last he returned to reality, he was stiff and cold and filled with a thousand aches and all the horror of returning fragments of memory.

The air was still and cold. There was a high, full moon. And nearby, there were two bodies lying familiarly close to each other on the grass. One was Camilla, the other a pre-pube—a boy of perhaps eleven or twelve. They had their hands tightly round each other's throat. They felt very cold.

Camilla's clothing had been torn to shreds. There were scratches and bruises all over her body, blood on her abdomen. Her mouth was wide open, her tongue protruded, and she stared in sightless wonder at the moon.

Numbly, Gabriel removed the prepube's hands from her throat. Numbly he raised her head, pressing it to his breast, kissing the damp hair, stroking the cold forehead, rocking back and forth as one long cry of anguish exploded from the depths of his being.

He sat there, cold, mindless and tormented, nursing Camilla, weeping and mumbling incomprehensible endearments to her while the moon passed slowly across the sky. He sat there nursing his dead love until the noise of a low, patrolling proc chopper jerked him back into the world of reality. He saw the proc chopper's searchlight sweeping systematically across the park.

Then he had the good sense to kiss Camilla for the last time very gently, gently lay her down—then run.

# CHAPTER TWENTY-EIGHT

Utterly traumatized, and without knowing how he accomplished it, Gabriel managed to make his way back to the apartment in Shepherd's Bush. Eustace was dead, and Camilla was dead, but P 939 went marching gaily on. It was all a joke. Dead funny. A monstrous joke conceived perhaps by some perverted supergitt upstairs to provide a few moments of divinely infernal amusement.

Gabriel wanted to laugh. He wanted to cry. He wanted to want to bang his head on the wall, cut his throat, destroy hordes of nameless prepubes. He could do nothing—because he was traumatized and insanely tranquil and horribly alone.

He began to drink. He did not eat, but he began to drink. Daylight came, then darkness, then more daylight, then more darkness. He went to sleep on the floor only when he was too drunk to stay conscious. He went to the bathroom only to pee or be sick. He went out of the apartment only to buy more vodka, whisky, gin, brandy or whatever.

He looked like a zombie. People avoided him in the street. The charlie at the wine shop wondered whether to call the procs, but Gabriel, a bleary-eyed automaton, dropped enough folding money to pay for the booze ten times over. The wine charlie did not call the procs but merely prayed for another visit soon.

Returning from one of his whisky forays, Gabriel literally bumped into Dr. Slink, returning bright-eyed, uplifted, renewed, purged and dedicated from a P.U.L. service personally conducted by Brother Peter who had emerged like a butterfly from the Karamazov caterpillar she had formerly known to become the Son of Man. The butterfly no longer seemed to have any connection at all with the caterpillar. Brother Peter was no more, no less than Brother Peter—the way to Perfect Universal Love.

Horrified by Gabriel's appearance, Dr. Slink managed to steer him into her apartment. She decided that he, too, could use a shot of Perfect Universal Love. At first Gabriel would not talk, or perhaps he had been struck dumb. Dr. Slink tried to get his wife, but there was no answer. So, intending to call the meds, she put Gabriel to bed after a fashion and tried to clean him up.

He was dirty and hairy and he smelled of sweat and urine, and he would not be separated from the whisky bottle clutched tightly in his hand. But Perfect Universal Love gave Dr. Slink the strength to cope.

She nursed him against her ample breast like a baby, while the whisky slopped over them both. Presently, miraculously, Gabriel began to speak. It was an act of confession —a drunken addendum to Supergitt's monstrous joke.

In slurred, barely comprehensible words, Gabriel told all. He told Dr. Slink how he had met Camilla. He told her about Eustace and the animals, and about P 939, and St.

Paul's and Epping Forest and InSex and the great crusade. He told Dr. Slink how he had deliberately infected her, and how the disease of non-aggression was spreading across the world. He told her how he and Camilla had gone for a walk in Kensington Gardens and how it had ended in the dirtiest most perverted joke Supergitt could devise.

Dr. Slink listened to his ramblings with a growing sense of wonder. Even exhilaration. There was a pattern—a divine pattern in it all. There had been purpose even in Dr. Perrywit's dismissal of Professor Greylaw. There had been purpose in Dr. Slink's chance encounter with Peter Karamazov in the park (she still did not know it had been Ilyich). There had been purpose also in Dr. Perrywit's sexual attack, and even in the ignominious dismissal from MicroWar. There was purpose in the never to be forgotten ecstasy she had experienced with Gabriel. There was purpose in everything. Suddenly she felt radiant with knowledge and wisdom and divine truth.

She stroked Gabriel's hair and pressed his face to her breast. And her eyes shone.

"Gabriel," she said softly, "you have told me terrible and horrible and wonderful things. You and Brother Peter have shown me how our lives—how all our lives—are bound together. And now, despite all these frightening events, the world is being conquered at last by peace and by love. The age of miracles is not past. God moves in mysterious ways."

Gabriel hiccupped and clumsily caressed her nipple without any enthusiasm at all. "God," he announced heavily, "is a Supergitt. God is a cosmic fart."

"God is Love," said Dr. Slink serenely.

"Crap!" retorted Gabriel, slopping more whisky down his chin and Dr. Slink's breast. "God is a noise in your head and a bug in your vagina ... All I know is that when I found something to love, it had to be taken away ... God's balls! Camilla is dead, you big bitch! Camilla is dead! Stopped, smashed, finished, kaput, gone!" He clutched Dr. Slink convulsively and began to sob. Her breast and half her body became drenched in tears and whisky. Presently, Gabriel slipped into unconsciousness.

But Dr. Slink did not call the meds. She had found compassion. With deadly dedication, with ruthless patience and with Perfect Universal Love, she set about nursing Gabriel back to health.

For three days he was too weak to resist. Then, on the fourth day, while Dr. Slink was out purchasing good, wholesome health foods, he crept out of her apartment, out of Margot Fonteyn House, and out of her life for ever.

# CHAPTER TWENTY-NINE

Gabriel did not know why he had returned to 1735, Babs-castle Boulevard. Gabriel did not know anything. Perhaps it was a sentimental journey. Perhaps he was chasing ghosts. Perhaps he was simply looking for tangible souvenirs of his lost love. Perhaps he was hoping that Supergitt would play another funny trick and turn back the clock, take the main-spring out of time, so that he could hold Camilla in his arms once more.

The house was deserted. The garden, where a squirrel, a lamb and a fat white rabbit had once frolicked with the big cats at night, was an overgrown desolation. Gabriel could not open the main door to the house, but he did not need to. Practically every window had been smashed—no doubt as the result of the tender attentions of prepubes or students.

Gabriel, carefully nursing a precious bottle of vodka, got in through one of the ground-floor windows, cutting himself slightly in the process. He went into the lounge. Surprisingly, it had not changed greatly since he had last seen it—was it months ago, years ago? Anyway, in another kind of time.

Something other than animals had knocked the grand piano about a bit, and curtains had been torn down from their hangings. But there were still rabbit and sheep droppings on what was left of the Indian carpet, there were still claw and tooth marks on the cocktail cabinet and the piano; and the settee looked as if it had wrestled with a panther or a lion yesterday. However, spiders had taken over. Presumably they had invaded from the garden; and now almost everywhere there was the fine tracery of webs that somehow locked everything in a lost pocket of time.

Gabriel did a quick tour of the house. It was a mistake to visit the bedroom where he and Camilla had first blissfully exhausted each other. The bed and wardrobe had been smashed, ransacked drawers pulled hastily from chests had been flung in all directions. Remnants of Camilla's clothing lay in absurd places, oddly mocking him.

It was a mistake also to visit the bathroom, where Gabriel had compulsively made love to Camilla on the floor before taking her away to escape the real or imagined attentions of the Security boyos. For a moment, as he surveyed the bathroom, Gabriel imagined he saw the two wet marks left by two wet bodies on the carpet. But when he inspected more closely, the marks were broad stains—possibly of blood. And quite possibly the result of some bizarre student caper.

He went downstairs once more into the lounge, and sat on the settee to drink vodka and wait a while for a ghost that would never come. After two deep swigs of vodka, he put the cork in the bottle and stretched arms that had been aching with sheer tension.

By chance, as he stretched, one of his hands slipped between the torn back of the settee and the tattered seat cushion. By chance, his hand encountered something thin and smooth. Automatically his fingers closed on it. He pulled it out. Gabriel had found an unposted letter. It was addressed to Camilla.

With suddenly shaking fingers, Gabriel opened the letter and began to read it.

"My darling wife," he read. "I am writing here what I lack the courage to say to you, and I shall arrange for this letter to be delivered when I am not at home. I am, as you know, a devout and professional coward; and I want you to have expended whatever emotion you may find it necessary to expend and reached whatever decisions you need to reach before I get back.

"You no doubt wonder why I intend to continue my work even though MicroWar has given me the push. And I am sure that now you are sober (yes, I did fix the drinks) you are wondering why I insisted on injecting you with P 939.

"Dearest, despite all my glib explanations on that intense and somewhat alcoholic evening, I did not inject you with P 939 either for the advancement of science or so that I could measure phase development in a human being. All that was gobbledegook.

"I injected you so that I could exert a very simple but, I hope, effective form of blackmail.

"You see, the trouble is that I love you very dearly. I know you do not love me and that I am no good at sex. But that does not matter. I am content to be with you, to know that I can watch Marilyn Monroe, that sad, gay child enchantress, and know that I, too, can hold her—you—in my arms with tenderness and sometimes even with passion.

"I know you do not love me, and that does not matter. What does matter is that I also know that you do not intend to renew our marriage contract, and that you will hold me to the agreement, take the money and just disappear.

"I could not bear to lose you. That is why I injected you (how I wish I could have done it the other way!) with P 939. Because now, my love, you need me as I need you.

"You see, until I have found an answer—and believe me, I am not very far off—the long-term effects of P 939 are disastrous, if not devastating.

"I first noticed what I call the cumulative eruption effect when I had a second generation rabbit living harmoniously with an infected fox at the zoo. One day I discovered that the rabbit (then mature after receiving P 939 in late adolescence) had kicked the fox to death. It was a great shock to me.

"I began to investigate—with mice, next time. I used mice because the mouse metabolism and life-cycle is comparatively fast, and I wanted quick results. I put a stray cat through to phase three, then I allowed it to live at the zoo with half a dozen infected white mice. I had done my arithmetic; and sure enough, within six hours of the predicted time, the mice attacked the cat. I checked the experiment, of course, and repeated it with other short-living, fast-breeding animals and was able to determine the operative cycle of P 939. I could not have done this with large animals, you understand, because it would all have taken too long. I was up against time—the time when you would take your money and go.

"But now, my darling, I hope it will be impossible for you to leave me. Because if you do, within four or five years you will become insanely violent. All the pent up aggression of the years of tranquillity will be released in one long murderous onslaught. Almost certainly you will become quite homicidal, and if you do not destroy yourself society will have to lock you away.

"Whereas, if you stay with me, I will *guarantee* to find an effective means of destroying the spirochete or neutralizing its long-term effect. Properly developed, P 939 can bring mankind to greatness. In its present state, it could be the most terrible scourge the world has ever known.

"Hate me, be indifferent to me, despise me. But please, my darling Camilla, my dearest Marilyn, do not leave me. I beg you to consider this problem calmly and to understand that only my great love for you could have driven me to such extremes. Your affectionate and loving husband—for always, I hope. Eustace."

Gabriel read the letter once, twice, three times. He was stunned. Eustace the comical genius was revealed as Eustace the fiendish fiend. P 939, the world-saver, was revealed as P 939, the universal annihilator. And the great crusade of peace was revealed as the super-colossal crusade of ultimate, absolute violence. Big, big joke.

Gabriel and Camilla and Messalina and every unconscious volunteer in the unknown army of salvation had slaved and copulated and gorged themselves and become frustratingly deadeningly non-aggressive all in vain.

Big Joke. BIG BIG JOKE!

That twisted Supergitt upstairs had excelled himself. This was the all-time greatest.

It was even funny enough to make you cry.

Gabriel cried. He cried and drank vodka, and cried and drank vodka, and then walked mindlessly away from the mausoleum that was 1735 Babscastle Boulevard, walking back into the poor, dear, doomed world of men.

# CHAPTER THIRTY

It was the suicide kick again. Standard routine. He had gone through it all before. But this time, Gabriel was determined to make it for real.

He had said goodbye to all his favourite landmarks, and now he stood once more in front of that gorgeously hideous nadir of nineteenth century aesthetics, the Albert Memorial. Also present was the raven. Perhaps it was the self-appointed custodian of the monument to Albert the Good. Perhaps it was the reincarnation of Disraeli or Gladstone or even some obscure but faithful gent of the royal bedchamber or some-such. Perhaps it was simply a figment of imagination. Whatever, if not a friend, it was at least a tolerable drinking companion.

Further, although it had not seen Gabriel for some considerable time, it clearly remembered former fond debaucheries; for it waddled towards him with thinly disguised enthusiasm.

Gabriel had remembered to bring two plastic cups. But no vodka, this time. It was an occasion for champagne—a magnum for himself and a magnum for the raven. No matter that the champagne was warm: it was the symbol that counted. He would briefly introduce the bird to gracious living before hopefully introducing himself to gracious dying. Waterloo Bridge and the Thames, definitely. And to hell with effluent!

"Greetings, feathery fantast," said Gabriel, expertly driving a champagne cork at the stoic figure of Prince Albert. "I bring you tidings of some interest. Mankind has had it. The entire planet is a human time-bomb. Homo Sap is destined to go round the twist, up the spout, down the shoot. We are constructing a world fit for ravens to live in. *Salud!*" He placed a brimming, bubbling cup of champagne on the stone step. The raven dipped its beak in, gratefully.

"I must apologize for the champers," went on Gabriel, himself taking a hearty draught. "Veuve Clicquot non-vintage. Also warm. Still, not unpleasing, I trust ... Where was I? Ah, yes. Featherbag, you should be grateful. We—that is I and a few thousand million other doomed members of my species—are preparing to sweep ourselves under the carpet. Quite possibly the last waltz will be a trifle noisy. But after the deluge—you. And all the other highly cunning, dimwitted creatures that have had neither the opportunity nor the inclination to meddle with the natural order of things. More champagne?"

"Kronk," said the raven.

Gabriel replenished both cups. "Still I discovered what it was like to love," he mused. "And he who loves last loves loudest. Bird, I loved loud. Let us drink to that."

The raven, also aware of a sense of occasion, dipped its beak once more.

"I may have lost out on book sculpture," went on Gabriel,

"but I have become something of an expert at delayed-action genocide. Of course, it was not exactly planned like that, but I will not weary you with details ... *Prost, Grüss Got, á votre santé* and bottoms up!" He knocked back the cup of champagne in one. The raven stared in admiration.

"I give you Gabriel's law," said Gabriel, filling his own cup once more. "Whosoever would save mankind shall fuck it up. *Salud!*"

Obediently the raven drank.

"And now," announced Gabriel, "before I get pissed out of my tiny mind, and while I am riding the crest of a non-vintage stimulus, I go to make a transient hole in what one may jokingly call the waters of the Thames. To you, dear drinking friend, I bequeath the rest of the Veuve Clicquot. May you remember me with some affection, and may the shakes sit lightly upon you. Look after Albert. He never said much, but I feel he was with us spiritually ... And now, that glorious line! For me, there is only one way out."

"Kronk," said the raven emphatically. "Kronk, Kronk." It flapped its wings a trifle unsteadily and regarded him with beady wisdom.

Gabriel met the raven's gaze. "What nonsense is this? Another way out? You lie, frowzy fowl, tell me you lie!"

"Kronk," said the raven, shaking its head. "Kronk ... Kronk ... Kronk!"

Gabriel gazed hard at the bird. Then he poured some more champagne, downed it, and gazed hard at the bird again. The raven met his gaze. It did not blink.

"Ha!" exclaimed Gabriel at length. "Eureka! I have it! And now I know how William Tell discovered gravity. All is not yet lost, is it, *mon vieux*? You have been trying to tell me, and you were right to try to tell me. And now I know. Supergitt, if humorous, is merciful. I had a reason for dying, and now I have a reason for living. And you have given it me, you generous, feathery fool. *Salud!*"

"Kronk," said the raven. Man and bird both drank deep.

"So instead of making a hole in the Thames," went on Gabriel, "I pop along to MicroWar and tell all. Then they tell America, Russia, etc. and pretty damn soon the world's scientists are united in their efforts to find the knock-out for P 939. Eustace Greylaw was no genius. What he can do, a million think tanks can undo. Eureka! Stay with the champers, matey. Have fun. I will return. *Salud!*"

"Kronk!" said the raven.

Gabriel staggered down the many steps of the Albert Memorial, oblivious of everything. He was filled with a terrible urgency. Before he could fall into alcoholic stupor, drop dead of a heart attack, fall down and break his neck, walk inadvertently into the Thames, or get killed on the road, he must get to MicroWar and tell all. Then the U.S. cavalry would ride over the hill, the heroine would be released from the railway track, the secret agent would not drown in the cellar. And all would be well.

Unfortunately, Gabriel forgot that the odds were stacked against him. They had always been stacked against him. Unfortunately, he forgot that Supergitt—if, indeed, Supergitt exists—must have a very odd sense of humour, beyond the imaginings of men. Unfortunately, he forgot that roads are designed to be used by traffic and that people with vital missions should not attempt to cross Knightsbridge in a state of heedless exaltation.

The hover sled was travelling at high speed. It hit Gabriel at high speed. It was driven—using the term loosely—by an intensely agitated Brother Peter, attempting to escape the hot pursuit of his campaign managers, public relations officers and accountants. With quite unwordly naïvety, he had committed the unforgivable indiscretion of publicly insisting that *all* the massive funds accumulated by the Perfect Universal

188

Love movement be devoted to purchasing comforters, diapers, feeding bottles and processed milk for one hundred million starving Chinese babies.

The hover sled hit Gabriel a glancing blow that spun him round three times and dropped him in a mangled heap in the gutter. Obeying Newtonian laws of motion with rough precision, Brother Peter executed three aerial somersaults and fell flat on his face. Both men were mortally injured.

Gabriel was still conscious. The world was filled with thunder. Or was it laughter? Laughter, most probably. Supergitt was having a ball.

He was aware of someone crawling towards him. A man he felt he ought to know but did not. Perhaps the joker was coming to help, though somehow Gabriel already knew that he was beyond help.

Nevertheless, human nature being incredibly stupid and sentimental, he stretched out a hand. Painfully, slowly, the other man pulled, crawled, willed himself forward. He, too, held out a hand. The hands touched.

"I bring you," gurgled Brother Peter, choking on his own blood, "the message of Perfect Universal Love."

Gabriel looked up. Suddenly he knew that the thunder really was laughter. And he knew where it came from.

With a tremendous effort, he managed to grip Brother Peter's hand, and held it tightly. There was a brief surge of kinship, a flicker of brotherhood.

Then Gabriel died ...

Laughing!

# EDMUND COOPER

## A FAR SUNSET

'Close to the first rank of writing in the genre'

*Irish Times*

The year-2032 A.D. The Gloria Mundi, a star ship built and manned by the new United States of Europe, touches down on the planet, Alatair Five. Disaster strikes, leaving only one apparent survivor – an Englishman named Paul Marlow, whose adventures in the lair of a strange primeval race known as the Bayani leads him firstly to their God, the omnipotent and omniscient Oruri, and eventually to an unlimited power that is so great that it must include a built-in death sentence. The forces that have remained static for centuries overcome both the forces of the future and the quest for unlimited knowledge.

'Well-told and moving'

*Sunday Telegraph*

'No question that the customer may not get his money's worth of adventure'

*Books and Bookmen*

**CORONET BOOKS**

**JACK VANCE**

**THE ANOME**

## DURDANE THE IMPRISONED

A world of strange ways and stranger people. A land where men and women are marked for life. Where they are bound to irrevocable destinies by the proclamations of the Faceless Man — an unseen power which terrorises and controls the world.

Durdane is a place where defiance is punished with death. But this kingdom of myriad mystery and incalculable peril is now threatened by a menace from without — the dreaded Rogushkoi. And only one youth, Gastel Etzwane, dares to challenge the unchallengeable, the power of the Faceless Man, in an extraordinary struggle for mastery and for the survival of Durdane . . .

**CORONET BOOKS**

# MORE SCIENCE FICTION FROM CORONET

☐ 04364 4
**EDMUND COOPER**
A Far Sunset 60p

**RICHARD AVERY**
☐ 19472 3 The Deathworms of Kratos 35p
☐ 19875 3 The War Games of Zelos 50p

**HOWARD FAST**
☐ 21009 5 A Touch of Infinity 70p

**ed DAMON KNIGHT**
☐ 19926 1 A Perchance to Dream 80p

**SAUL DUNN**
☐ 20790 6 Steeleye — The Wideways 60p
☐ 21003 6 Steeleye — Waterspace 50p

**JACK VANCE**
☐ 19830 3 The Asutra 75p
☐ 19827 3 The Anome 75p
☐ 20820 1 The Gray Prince 60p
☐ 19828 1 The Brave Free Men 75p

*All these books are available at your local bookshop or newsagent,*
*or can be ordered direct from the publisher. Just tick the titles you*
*want and fill in the form below.*

Prices and availability subject to change without notice.

---

CORONET BOOKS, P.O. Box 11, Falmouth, Cornwall.
Please send cheque or postal order, and allow the following for
postage and packing:
U.K. — One book 22p plus 10p per copy for each additional book
ordered, up to a maximum of 82p.
B.F.P.O. and EIRE — 22p for the first book plus 10p per copy for the
next 6 books, thereafter 4p per book.
OTHER OVERSEAS CUSTOMERS — 30p for the first book and 10p
per copy for each additional book.

Name ....................................................................................

Address ................................................................................

....................................................................................